THE SOGGY CANNOLI MURDER

AN ITALIAN-AMERICAN COZY MYSTERY SERIES
BOOK 1

M.P. BLACK

Copyright © 2023 by Mathias Black (writing as M.P. Black)

Published by MP Black Media

All rights reserved.

No part of this book may be reproduced in any form or by any electronic or mechanical means, including information storage and retrieval systems, without written permission from the author, except for the use of brief quotations in a book review.

Cover designed by GetCovers

For A.—I'll always be moonstruck by you

1

"You got a death wish?"

Mark Lewis, owner of Cafe Roma, shouldered me aside. He grabbed the portafilter handle out of my hand and yanked it from the espresso machine. Then he knocked the coffee back into the bucket with fresh grounds and quickly refilled it, tamping down one shot instead of two. Standing this close to him, I caught a whiff of alcohol off his breath.

"I told you, one shot of espresso per coffee."

"But the woman ordered an Americano," I said, keeping my voice low since the woman in question stood only a few feet away at the cafe counter waiting for her coffee. "She'll need two shots of espresso."

"She'll get one," he said.

He ran the ancient espresso machine. It roared and shook as one shot of ink-black coffee splashed into the white ceramic cup. Then Mark added hot water from the wand until it threatened to spill over the rim.

I watched with a mix of amazement and horror. The Americano was so watery, I could see the bottom through the murky liquid. You'd be forgiven if you thought it was a cup of tea.

"That's not an Americano," I said. "That's water with a whisper of coffee."

"If you want to waste your own money, that's fine. But don't waste mine. There's about 32 shots of espresso to a pound of coffee beans. Cut that in half and I can make my current inventory last another three months."

I was confused. "What happens in three months?"

"Nothing," he snapped. "The point is, I'm not in the business of giving my money away to customers. *Capisce*?"

This wasn't the first time this morning that Mark had peppered his speech with Italian. He was about as Italian as the Mayflower. But apparently it was part of his act—after all, Cafe Roma, like the entire town of Carmine, was supposed to be quintessentially Italian-American.

He stood back and folded his arms across his chest, eyeing me critically.

"Do you want this job or not?"

I bit my lip. Mark Lewis was a terrible boss and his cafe was a disaster. The espresso machine coughed up coffee as if it were dying. Mold spread across the ceiling. Water damage had warped and cracked the laminate floors, making more than one customer wrinkle their nose and turn away at the door.

And yes, my number one wish was to work here.

I nodded.

"Well, this job interview isn't over yet," he said, a gleam in his eye. He seemed to enjoy watching me squirm. He picked up the cup and handed it to me, and none too gently, either. Coffee sloshed over the edges.

"Here," he said. "Go serve her."

"*Va bene*, boss," I mumbled, and his eyes narrowed.

"*Va* what?"

I figured that if he could serve up Italian phrases, so could I. Though I might have sprinkled it with a little too much sarcasm.

In my defense, it was hard to get on board with the fake tribute to Italy that was Cafe Roma's bread and butter. But that was where the money was, according to Mark. New Yorkers, in particular, loved it. Carmine was called the "Little Italy" of New Jersey's distant Wessex County, and if out-of-towners bothered to come this far, it was to indulge in Italian-American culture.

As I went back to serving the customer, Mark settled down on a chair in the corner—hidden from customer view by the bulky, rust-fringed espresso machine—and picked up a dog-eared paperback, a chunk of its cover ripped off at the bottom. It was entitled *A Moron's Step-by-Step Guide to Living with Less*.

Somehow, it wasn't a surprising reading choice given his stinginess.

The gray-haired woman who had ordered the Americano had also asked for a cannoli. I slid the coffee cup and plate with the pastry toward her. She eyed both coffee and cannoli with suspicion, and frankly, so did I.

The cannoli had recently been wrapped in plastic and deep frozen, but the microwave in the cafe's back-room kitchen had remedied that. It was so soggy that it had deflated and half melted onto the plate.

The woman sighed, but she laid a wrinkled 5-dollar bill on the counter, the price of the coffee and cannoli special. Then grabbed her coffee cup and plate and found a seat by the window. In a moment, she was engrossed in a newspaper.

I checked the time on my phone. It was 11 am, three

hours after the cafe's regular opening time. Apart from the window seats running along the left-hand side, where the woman sat, the long, narrow cafe had four tiny tables pressed up against the right-hand wall. They were empty. The woman was the only customer.

The woman had chosen the best spot at the cafe's wall-length windows. Beyond where the woman sat, I got a good view of Garibaldi Avenue, Carmine's main drag, as well as Poplar Street, which ran down along Cafe Roma.

I leaned on the counter, staring out at the small town that was supposed to be my new home. It was Monday morning. Cars drifted up and down Garibaldi and people wandered to work or rushed to take care of morning errands.

On the opposite corner of Poplar and Garibaldi, a woman came out of Parisi & Parisi, Attorneys at Law, and pulled up the rolling steel shutters, opening for business. A bright yellow bicycle whizzed past. All down the street, bunting stretched from lamp post to lamp post, festooning Garibaldi Avenue with small Italian and U.S. flags.

I wondered if this place would ever feel like home, if I'd ever feel settled again.

"Excuse me."

The gray-haired woman interrupted my thoughts. She approached the counter, carrying the coffee cup and the plate. She set them both down with a grimace.

"I'm sorry, but I simply must speak up."

She made it sound like she was doing her civic duty. Guessing what she'd complain about, I didn't disagree.

"This Americano is so weak, it hardly tastes like coffee, and honestly, you should be ashamed of this cannoli. It's nothing like the photos you advertise outside." She gestured toward the sidewalk sign outside the cafe entrance. "If I didn't know better, I'd think this was a frozen cannoli that had been heated in a microwave. I can't eat this."

I apologized profusely, feeling the very shame she'd told me I ought to feel—multiplied by ten. There was right and there was wrong, and false advertising was squarely in the "wrong" category. I offered to get her another baked good and a fresh cup of coffee.

"Never mind the pastry," she said. "Coffee's all I want."

I removed her cup and the plate with the half-eaten cannoli, and I turned to make a fresh Americano.

Mark lowered his paperback. He placed a folded sheet of legal paper into the book to mark his place and glared at me.

"What do you think you're doing?"

"I'm making that woman another cup of coffee."

"Did she pay for another?"

"No, but—"

"Then why is she getting another? Is Cafe Roma a charity?"

"This coffee"—I stubbornly stood my ground—"is too weak. The cannolis you serve are soggy. And if we want customers to come back, we'll need to make sure they like the food and drinks, right?"

Mark gave me a long, hard glare. It seemed to be his favorite form of communication, and I guessed he'd had years of practice.

It did not make him attractive.

The crazy thing was that under different circumstances, he would have been a handsome forty-something-year-old. He had a finely cut jaw and a pair of arresting green eyes that would have made a casting agent look twice at him. But despite my Hollywood experience, or maybe because of it, I believed people's faces meant less than their hearts. Mark could have been a supermodel and his personality would still make him ugly.

Finally, when he thought his glare had done its damage, he said, "If she won't pay for the coffee, then you will."

"Wait, what?"

"You heard me, Bernie. The woman can pay for another coffee if she wants it. Or you can fork out the money. I sure as hell won't cover it."

"But—"

I stopped myself. *Drop it*, I thought. *It was your pigheaded belief in right or wrong that landed you in this mess in the first place. And this town.*

"Your resume, assuming it's true, says you're an experienced barista."

He pulled the folded piece of paper from his shirt pocket and opened it. Through the paper, I could see my name at the top, the false one I'd been given: Bernie Smyth.

"Even if you lied about your experience, you'd better start acting like one. Think you can do that?"

"I can do that," I said through gritted teeth.

Because yes, indeed, I could act.

He returned to reading his book, mumbling something about paying too much in wages. He pulled open the cupboard beneath the espresso machine and produced a small metal hip flask, which he took a swig from.

That explained why he reeked of alcohol.

I returned my attention to the customer and her fresh cup of coffee.

My experience as a barista wasn't entirely untrue, though admittedly a little "amplified" on my resume. Before I had my breakthrough as an actress, I worked at a coffee van in Los Angeles. It was a simple little truck, with only three drinks on offer: Americano, cappuccino, and latte.

Even leaving aside that bit of experience, I knew what a good cup of coffee ought to taste like. I had standards.

And I could be pretty stubborn about those standards.

So I made the gray-haired woman an Americano the way I'd learned to: two shots of espresso and hot water, the crema coating the surface. It felt good to make the coffee the way it ought to be made, and when the woman picked up the cup and took a sip and smiled, her joy warmed my insides.

"Ah," she said. "Much better, thanks."

We smiled at each other and I thought, *Hey, maybe this gig will work out after all.*

As the woman returned to her seat by the window, I saw she'd left her newspaper on the counter. I was about to call out to her, when a jolt, like electric shock, shot through me.

The newspaper had been folded to the front of the Entertainment section and there, in a large photo spanning the page, was my face. The headline said, "Death of America's Top TV Show Silver & Gold: Jay Casanova in prison, Bernadette Kovac STILL missing."

They'd picked a promotional photo from the last season of *Silver & Gold*. My character, Eve Silver, was standing back to back with Adam Gold, played by Jay Casanova. It was a shock to see him. I had avoided the news since the big trial, and the last time I saw him, he had been screaming at me across the courtroom as guards handcuffed him: "I'll get you for this, Bernadette—you'll regret your lies."

They hauled him off to prison while a team of U.S. Marshalls whisked me away, an unexpected end to America's most popular TV show, not to mention my acting career.

"Junk," Mark said, and I jumped. "TV these days is nothing but trash."

He leaned over and jabbed a finger at the photo.

"No one will miss that show any more than they'll miss those rotten actors."

I hoped he was right. If nobody missed the stars of *Silver & Gold*, then they also wouldn't notice the similarities between Bernadette Kovac and Bernie Smyth. I wore my hair short now, and my natural color—raven black—was strikingly different from Eve Silver's blonde curls. Besides, who would guess that Bernie Smyth, working a minimum wage job at a cafe in New Jersey, had anything to do with the famous actress?

Mark glared at the photo in the newspaper, picking it up for a closer look.

"What else have I seen that actress in? A movie? She looks familiar..."

My heart beat faster.

"She used to be everywhere. You've probably seen her in magazines and in ads and in TV commercials..."

"I guess so..."

He continued to study the photo.

Then, abruptly, he threw the paper down.

"All right, Bernie Smyth. You've got the job."

He held out a keychain with two keys.

My heart did a little somersault. "What? I do?"

"If you still want it."

"I do, I do."

I took the keychain. He explained one was the key to the front, the other to the back. Later, he'd show me where to put the garbage in the back alley.

He looked at his wristwatch. "Right now, I'm going out for lunch. You keep an eye on things."

I nodded, hardly able to absorb the good news. I got a job. This was a big step toward finding some kind of stability, while also keeping my identity a secret.

"I'll be back in an hour or two," Mark said.

But before he left, he cast another frown at the newspaper on the counter.

"Hmm..."

He grabbed a pen that lay on the cash register and he drew a large circle around Eve Silver's face. Next to it, he put a question mark: "?"

"I'm sure I'll remember where I've seen her."

I nodded mechanically, no words coming out. My mouth had gone dry. If he did remember, I was in deep trouble.

After Mark left, I realized I didn't know what to do if I ran out of change. I remembered a lack of quarters as being a particular problem back when I'd worked in the coffee van in L.A. I also didn't know what to do if I ran out of milk.

I pushed open the door to the back room. It served as both kitchen and storage. Boxes dominated the cramped space, some with bags of coffee and other supplies, but just as many empty. A fridge proved stocked with enough milk to last awhile. The freezer next to it was full of frozen cannolis and muffins. A long stainless steel counter included a wide sink and a workspace with a knife rack and a microwave. The microwave, an ugly beige-and-brown monstrosity, must have been one of the first ever produced. A frayed electricity cord ran out the back, its wiring exposed. Next to it hung a fire extinguisher, as if whoever installed it knew which appliance was most likely to explode first.

But earlier I'd used it to heat a cannoli, and it worked.

At the back was another door. I unlocked it and stuck my head out. The door led into a narrow alley with garbage cans, apparently running behind all the businesses on Garibaldi Avenue. To the right, I could see Poplar Street and the alley on the other side, which must be the backside of Parisi & Parisi, the law firm.

A woman came walking up Poplar, limping a little as she hurried past. Dark hair. Facial features tight with anger. Someone shouted from behind her. I recognized the voice. It was Mark's.

"Maria, you stupid—"

As the woman disappeared from view, I caught sight of Mark hurrying up the street. He also caught sight of me and he glared.

I quickly ducked back inside, shutting the door behind me.

Whatever Mark's fight was with that woman—and it had looked like a serious fracas—it was private, and I didn't want to appear to be spying on them.

I locked the door once more.

When I returned to the cafe, the gray-haired woman had left, but I had two new customers waiting by the counter.

Both were young guys, probably in their late twenties. One had fair hair, which fell over his round, steel-rimmed glasses. He swept his bangs aside and smiled.

"We heard there was a new barista at Cafe Roma," he said. "But seeing is believing."

The other guy was gazing at me. It made my skin crawl. He seemed to study me, calculating, as if I were a code to be cracked.

"Where are you from?" he asked. "What brings you to Carmine?"

The one with the glasses laughed.

"Don't mind Peter. He's a journalist and always looking for a big scoop."

I shuddered. A big scoop. Great. I could imagine the clickbait headline now: "Missing actress who put Jay Casanova in jail is hiding in this small New Jersey town." What could compete with that kind of scoop?

"Media entrepreneur, not just journalist," Peter said with pursed lips, as if the correction was one he was tired of having to make. "I'm the founder and editor of *The Carmine Enquirer*, Carmine's premier news source."

"Carmine's only news source." The guy with the glasses stuck out his hand. "I'm Nat. I work at the Carmine Historical Society. Peter handles the present; I take care of the past."

I shook his hand and introduced myself, using my assumed identity, of course.

Peter shook my hand, too. "Peter Piatek." He wouldn't let go of my hand. "So, Bernie Smyth, tell me about yourself."

"Nothing to tell," I said, trying to sound casual and confident. I stared straight at Peter. "I'm from out west, but this is home now."

I wrested my hand free from his.

"Any comment on Carmine? Maybe we'll run a story on a newcomer's perspective on our little Italian oasis."

"Peter, give her a break. She's new to town."

Peter ignored Nat.

"Rumor has it that Mark wants to sell the cafe. Any truth to that?"

Nat shook his head, apparently amused by his pushiness. "Peter likes nothing better than to snoop, and has done so *incessantly* ever since middle school. *The Carmine Enquirer* is just an excuse to do what he's always done."

"True, I've always had an *enquiring* mind," Peter said, smiling.

"Well, may I enquire..." I asked, eager to change topics, "...what kind of coffee you'd like?"

"Espresso, please. I know what happens to Americanos in this place." He gave me a smug smile. "It's my business to know these little things."

"Like the cannolis," I said.

He raised an eyebrow. "What about the cannolis?"

"Oh, we don't talk about the cannolis," Nat said with a smile. He winked at me. "Do we, Bernie?"

I returned his smile. "No, we don't."

Peter frowned. "Fine, keep your secrets."

I was glad to have an ally in warding off Peter's questions, and when Nat also ordered an espresso, I got busy preparing the coffees.

Standing behind the hulk of the espresso machine, I glanced over at Peter. He had long, straight hair, gathered in a ponytail. He wore a button-down shirt, neatly tucked into a pair of khakis, and a pair of leather shoes. In contrast, Nat wore a tie-dyed t-shirt over jeans and a pair of sneakers.

Suddenly, the espresso machine coughed and spluttered, and the inky stream of coffee reduced to a trickle.

"Oh, no," I said, a knot twisting in my gut. "The machine broke."

"No, it didn't," Nat said. He leaned over the counter and formed a fist, then walloped the machine on the side. It coughed again, and reluctantly, it seemed, rumbled back to life, spitting out coffee again.

"Thanks," I said, relief washing over me. What a disaster it would have been if the machine had broken on my first day on the job. "How did you know how to fix it?"

"I used to work here," Nat said. "Before Mark fired me."

"He what? Why?"

"Mark doesn't like anybody. Eventually he finds a reason

to fight with people, and if they happen to be his employees, he'll fire them." Nat spoke without anger or bitterness, as if he were stating the simple facts of life. "Nobody's survived long at Cafe Roma. He even fired Susan, his own cousin and one of his only relatives. And he did it when she desperately needed money. He doesn't care about anyone but himself."

A weight pressed down on my shoulders. I served Nat and Peter their espressos, trying to ignore that the thin ice I was crossing just cracked. But how could I ignore the idea that Mark, whose job I desperately needed, ultimately fired everyone? How long before he threw me out? What if he found out who I really was and wanted to make it a problem? Would I soon need to leave Carmine and find a new town to hide in?

Nat and Peter downed their espressos and said their goodbyes. But Peter stopped in the doorway, looked back at me, and said, "In a small town like Carmine, no one can keep their secrets for very long…"

Then Nat grabbed his friend by the arm and hauled him out of the cafe.

I buried my head in my hands. A local historian and a journalist snooping around me. A boss who hated everyone and might actually have recognized me. My new life in Carmine wasn't going to be easy.

THE NEXT MORNING, after a quick breakfast, I called Cafe Roma.

I had gone to bed with heart palpitations, but after waking up, I'd decided that my fate was in my own hands. Mark hadn't fired me yet. He hadn't discovered my true identity. Until he did either of those things, I was going to prove to him I was a one-in-a-million barista, an employee-of-the-year kind of woman, a killer asset.

After listening to the phone ring a few times, I wondered whether Mark hadn't arrived yet. Yesterday, he'd told me he lived above the cafe and went downstairs at the crack of dawn every day for a cappuccino.

Bright sunlight streamed through my little kitchen window. I looked at the clock on the side of my fridge.

6:00 am.

Maybe too early on a Tuesday morning?

My eyes drifted down to the old pizza boxes and empty soda cans on the counter, evidence of my sad life.

Mark answered the phone.

"Yeah, what do you want?"

I explained I was going to arrive by about 6:30 am, and that I wanted to do some tidying in the storage room before the regular work started.

"So you're coming in early. So what? Don't expect more pay."

"I won't," I said, forcing myself to sound chipper. "See you soon, boss."

But he'd already hung up. He sounded about as cheerful as ever.

I didn't let his abrasive personality get me down. Instead, I put on my shoes and slipped out of my house, locking the front door behind me.

I lived in a small, ranch-style house on Lampedusa Lane. The rent was reasonable—a steal compared with what I was used to back in L.A.—but it would still be a stretch on my barista salary. The money from the U.S. Marshalls Service would keep me afloat for a while, but soon they'd stop paying out, and I'd be on my own.

A lone car, an early commuter, drifted past me as I

turned onto Da Vinci Street. Gazing across lawns, I saw that most curtains and shades remained drawn. Behind them, I imagined, grown-ups and kids were digging into bowls of cereal, getting ready for the day ahead.

Birds sang in the sycamore trees. Leaves whispered in the breeze. The sun was warm, and the day's humidity was already gathering in the air.

I turned from Da Vinci Street onto Garibaldi Avenue. My mind had been so focused on the job yesterday that I hadn't appreciated how pretty the town center was: the lamp posts with planters overflowing with cheerful flowers; the banner strung across the street that said, "*Benvenuti* — Welcome!" in a nod to the town's Italian heritage; the red-checkered curtains in Moroni's Italian Bakery.

The delicious scent of baked sugar wafted out from the bakery, drawing me toward the window. The sign said it was closed, but apparently the baker was already at work. I held a hand over my eyes, shading them, and looked through the window.

Inside, a long glass counter glowed, spotlighting mounds of cookies and cakes. I licked my lips. My mouth was actually watering. I made a promise to myself to return to Moroni's, and only hoped I could afford a few cookies on my meagre wages.

I turned away from the bakery.

The street was deserted at this hour. Diagonally across Garibaldi Avenue sat Cafe Roma. Its roof sagged. The second-floor windows were dark, the curtains drawn. Mark would be downstairs in the cafe.

I steered toward Cafe Roma. The rolling steel shutters were three-quarters of the way up, enough to allow me to duck under and get through the front door, but still obscuring the interior of the cafe.

I jiggled the key in the lock. I could unlock it, yet the door didn't budge.

It must still be bolted on the inside.

I knocked.

"Mark?" I called out. "It's me, Bernie. The door is bolted."

No answer came. But a moment later, I heard a clatter. Somewhere a door slammed. I waited and knocked again and then decided to try my luck with the back door.

I walked around the building. The shutters were all the way down on the Poplar Street side. Across the way, Parisi & Parisi was equally closed up.

Poplar Street continued down a slight incline and, quickly leaving Garibaldi Avenue's commerce behind, entered a residential neighborhood.

In the narrow alley behind Cafe Roma, I slipped past the garbage cans and tugged at the back door's handle. It was locked. I dug out the keys and shoved the right one in the lock.

The door swung open.

Good thing it wasn't bolted from the inside.

The kitchen was as messy as ever, with balled-up paper towel on the counter and empty cartons of milk left standing by the sink.

Well, this morning I'd roll my sleeves up and impose some order on this chaos.

"Mark?"

I wrinkled my nose. Was something burning?

I stepped past the empty boxes and the work counter, pushing open the door to the cafe.

A bunch of keys lay on the counter. And next to that, a coffee cup. It looked like an unfinished cappuccino, Mark's preferred morning beverage, and there was a small, round smudge next to it.

But as I stepped forward, I forgot all about these details, because beyond the counter, near the first cafe table, lay a body. And it was on fire.

I stood rooted to the spot.

Flames danced from Mark's back.

I recognized him at once. I also recognized one of the sharp knives from the kitchen.

Someone had buried it in his back. Then set fire to him.

My feet wouldn't move. They seemed nailed to the floor. It wasn't until an image of Jay Casanova yelling at me flashed through my mind that I tore myself free.

I jumped back, threw myself through the kitchen door, and grabbed the fire extinguisher. The canister was heavy. As I hurtled back into the cafe, I pulled out the pin and aimed the nozzle at Mark's body and squeezed the handle. White foam shot out and I swiveled the nozzle back and forth until I was sure the fire was out.

I put down the canister and crouched next to the body. There was no doubt he was dead.

I suddenly felt cold and hugged myself.

A murder investigation, I thought. *It's about the worst thing that could happen.*

The cops would dig into my past. That journalist, Peter Piatek, he would dig, too. There was no way they wouldn't find out. The entire world would know my secret. And then the danger that had chased me across the country would catch up with me.

I couldn't let that happen.

I looked around. What had I touched? The fire extinguisher. The door handle.

Before I could explain to myself what I was doing, I'd found a rag behind the counter to wipe off my prints. Since the foam was all over the place, I left the fire extinguisher where it was.

I backed out of the cafe. I wiped the back door's handle and carefully locked it again, hoping I'd remembered to leave everything the way I'd found it.

Except the body, of course.

Jeez, Bernie, what are you doing?

For a moment, I hesitated by the back door.

This is wrong...

There was right and there was wrong. But there was also staying alive. I'd get out of here and call the cops and report the murder. I couldn't tell them much, anyway.

They were the professionals. They'd figure it out.

I pocketed the keys and turned to leave.

"Freeze," the police officer said.

She'd pulled her gun and was pointing it at me.

"Ferrante," she called out. "Back here. Looks like we caught the perp."

2

Chief of Police Diana Tedesco, with her hands on the table in the interrogation room, towered over me. She had an unflattering bowl cut with streaks of wiry gray and deep shadows beneath her eyes, made even deeper by the fluorescent lights overhead.

The chair I sat on must have been designed for discomfort. No matter how I arranged myself, everything hurt: my butt, my back, my legs. At least they hadn't handcuffed me.

"Things don't look so good for you," Chief Tedesco said in a raspy voice. "Why don't you come clean and tell us the truth?"

The other police officer—Ferrante—leaned against the door, his arms across his chest. He was about my age, early thirties, and had the perfect combination of muscular build with rugged, handsome features. A romantic lead. An action hero. Under different circumstances, I might have spent my time looking at him. But Chief Tedesco held my attention.

"I've told you the truth."

"All right. Tell me again."

I sighed. This would be the fifth time I repeated my

story. Was Chief Tedesco making me tell the story over and over in the hopes that I would make a mistake, reveal the actual truth behind my lies? I recognized the technique. It was one my character, Eve Silver, had used to break down criminals.

I told her once more about my decision to go to work early, describing my brief conversation with Mark on the phone.

"He was alive at 6:11 am," I said. "He was dead when I got to the cafe around 6:30 am."

"He was certainly dead after you left the cafe."

I groaned inwardly and slumped in my seat. In hindsight, my panicked decision to run from the scene of the crime had been reckless and insane, and I'd told the cops as much.

"You knew your boss would be at the cafe. You had keys, so you could sneak through the back door and surprise him."

"I didn't sneak anywhere," I said. "The front was locked, and I banged on the door and called Mark's name." Suddenly, a jolt went through my body as a memory came back to me. I sat up straight. "Wait, I just remembered something. After I knocked on the front door, I heard a door slam. Maybe it was the killer leaving through the back."

"Convenient that you should remember that now."

"Look," I said. "I know how it looks, me running away and all. But I tried to put out the fire using the fire extinguisher."

Chief Tedesco smiled and pushed away from the table. She paced the floor.

"Did you know that Mark Lewis drank?"

I couldn't see why we'd moved onto this topic. I nodded.

"Sure. I saw him drink from a hip flask. He smelled of alcohol."

"I'll admit you were smart, Miss Smyth. You had all the murder weapons at your disposal: a sharp knife from the kitchen and a hip flask full of bourbon. By pouring his own booze over him and then setting him on fire, you increased the chances that any DNA evidence would be wiped out. Smart. But the fire extinguisher was a stroke of genius. By dousing the body with foam, you made it 100 percent certain that forensics could find nothing."

"This is insane. I didn't kill Mark Lewis. What motive could I possibly have for killing my new boss? I was grateful to get the job."

Chief Tedesco turned to Officer Ferrante. "Did you hear that, Ferrante? 'Motive.' She's studied her cop shows on TV and thinks she knows a thing or two about our business."

I frowned. "That's not what I was suggesting…"

Chief Tedesco spun around, pointing a finger at me. "A witness came forward and told us you had an altercation with Mark Lewis."

"An altercation?"

My mind spun, leaving me dizzy. I thought back to the brief time I'd spent with Mark, but I couldn't make sense of it—what did she mean by "altercation"?

"Yes," she said. "A heated argument about a cannoli."

"A what?"

Chief Tedesco consulted a file on the table, flipping through the pages.

"Yes, a soggy cannoli."

This time, I groaned aloud. "Oh, come on. We had a disagreement about coffee and cannolis. I felt strongly—"

She leaned closer. "How strongly, Miss Smyth? Strongly enough to—"

I cut her off. "—that if you order an Americano, you should get a decent Americano. And if you order a cannoli, you should get a decent cannoli."

"I'm sure you're an expert on how cannoli should be prepared. I'm sure you—"

I shot to my feet.

"Mark Lewis served frozen cannolis that had been microwaved so badly that they melted on the plate."

The room fell into a deep hush. Chief Tedesco's eyes widened, and she turned from me, silently consulting Officer Ferrante. He grimaced, reacting with obvious distaste to the revelation.

"Ferrante," she barked. "Go check."

He left the room.

She turned back to me.

"Sit."

I did as she told me, my body crying out at being returned to the uncomfortable seat.

A moment later, Officer Ferrante, with his chiseled jawline, reappeared in the doorway. Chief Tedesco joined him and they whispered. I watched her scratch the back of her neck and heard the words "soggy cannoli" again and Ferrante add more audibly, "Well, anyone in their right mind would stand up for that."

Anger welled up in me, only tempered by a bone-aching weariness. This was ridiculous. My innocence was at stake, and they took the quality of a cannoli more seriously than my testimony. But I wouldn't sit here all day and suffer this absurd interrogation. I knew I had certain rights. Eve Silver was no slouch when it came to the law.

I took a deep breath. "Are you arresting me?"

Chief Tedesco frowned.

"Because if you are," I said, "I'd like to talk to a lawyer."

Chief Tedesco's frown threatened to cave in her entire face. "All the evidence points to you, Miss Smyth. I caught you fleeing the scene of the crime. You claim you snuck through the back, because the front door was locked. But no one can corroborate your story. No one can—"

"Uh, chief."

Officer Ferrante gestured for his boss to join him by the door. Another officer had joined them. They conferred in whispers with several ahs, uhs, and one sharp intake of breath from Chief Tedesco.

When she turned around, her face blazed bright red and the corners of her mouth dipped in bitter anger.

"It seems," she said, her tone icy, "that a witness has come forward saying she saw you at the front door of Cafe Roma at 6:30 am, and heard you knock and call Mark's name."

I studied her for a moment, expecting more. When she said nothing, I did: "So you're not arresting me."

She gave a curt shake of her head.

"You'll need to stay in town. We will have more questions. Ferrante, get a cruiser and drive Miss Smyth back home."

Officer Ferrante and the other cop left the doorway, and for a moment I was alone with Chief Tedesco.

I made a move to stand.

She slammed her hand down on the tabletop, and I jumped. We stared across the table at each other.

"You're not fooling me," she hissed.

She pulled something from the folder on the table and slid it in front of me. It was a newspaper. An invisible hand squeezed my heart hard as I recognized the page with the photograph of me and Jay Casanova. Eve Silver and Adam Gold. And Mark's note. He had circled the photograph and, next to it, written a question mark: "?"

"I know who you are," she said in a low voice. "And I think Mark did, too. That's why you killed him. And I'm going to prove it."

FROM OFFICER FERRANTE'S CRUISER, I watched the streets of Carmine roll past me, and wondered what had gone wrong. This town was supposed to be my haven, not another danger to contend with.

Ferrante turned onto Garibaldi Avenue, and we drifted past Cafe Roma. Crime scene tape stretched across the front door.

I could sense Ferrante glancing at me, but I was in no mood to talk. I'd spent the past five hours talking.

"Everything will be all right," he said.

When I didn't respond, he added, "Don't worry. Chief Tedesco will solve the case and catch the killer."

That was exactly what I was worried about—only the killer, in her mind, was me.

"Meanwhile, you ought to get to know Carmine."

"I've already seen enough," I grumbled.

"You mean Cafe Roma? That place is a dump. And let's agree that the interrogation room at our police department isn't much fun, either."

I glanced over at him, and sure enough, he was smiling. The guy got points for being nice.

"You just need to meet the good people of Carmine and you'll love it here."

I gave a noncommittal grunt. Good people? I thought of Peter Piatek and his incessant questions. I thought of Mark

Lewis with a knife in his back. Maybe I'd already had enough of the good people of Carmine.

"You need someone who can show you around town," Ferrante said, giving me a sidelong glance. "Make you feel at home."

I raised an eyebrow at him. "And that person happens to be you?"

He smiled. It was a big, boyish grin, and impossible to ignore. My heart did an annoying little flutter. *Not now, Heart,* I told it. But did it listen?

"I can show you Lake Carmine and the trails through the woods. And the Overlook. Amazing views. Plus, I can take you to the Old Mill. That's a bar. Best bar in the world, and it's *the* place to hang out in Carmine. You can meet absolutely everyone."

I had been warming to the idea until he said that word, "everyone." I shook my head.

"I don't like an audience," I said.

That had been my mistake from the get-go. I should never have let my U.S. Marshall convince me to work in a cafe where I would be exposed to so many people every day. Maybe baristas were anonymous in big cities like Los Angeles or New York, just another face filling a coffee order, but in a small place like Carmine, I couldn't hide.

No, I didn't want to meet "everyone." And I didn't want another job at a cafe. My next job would be in a call center or a warehouse, somewhere I could hide.

Unless, of course, Chief Tedesco got me a job printing license plates in a prison.

I sighed. I had to leave this town and find a new place.

We drove up Da Vinci Street. Sprinklers waved water across bright green lawns. A dog walker with three eager

Dalmatians tripped down the sidewalk. A pair of sneakers hung from a tree branch overhead, the victim of a prank.

Everything looked beautifully, wonderfully ordinary.

As Ferrante turned onto Lampedusa Lane, he said, "Looks like you've got a package."

The palms of my hands tingled. In my driveway stood a USPS truck, and I knew at once that it wasn't a mail delivery.

3

Closing the front door behind me, I waited in the hallway for a moment, listening to the police cruiser drive down the street.

The short hallway led straight to the kitchen and living-room combo. To the right were two doors, each leading to a small bedroom.

"Roberta?" I called out.

"In the kitchen," she answered.

U.S. Marshall Roberta LaRosa sat at my kitchen table drinking coffee out of my mug. My mug had a drawing of three Hollywood Walk of Fame stars, below which it said, "When it is dark enough, you can see the stars." Somehow, the saying comforted me. Guess I'd been feeling life was pretty gloomy.

Roberta shook her head, looking down at the cup with disgust. "Instant coffee? You're a barista for crying out loud, and all you've got for me is instant coffee? Your fridge is no better."

I went to the fridge. Looking inside, I was struck by how sad it looked. A couple of bags of pre-washed lettuce. A bottle of Italian dressing. Some seltzer water. A row of ginger ales. Otherwise empty, so empty.

I'd been living off frozen pizza and soda while binge-watching old episodes of *House* and *Murder, She Wrote* and *Remington Steele*. My life was empty, so empty.

I turned to Roberta. "I can't stay in Carmine."

"Because your boss was murdered?"

"For starters, yes."

I bristled. Her cool, unflappable tone bothered me. Mark got stabbed and set on fire, and she was upset about my instant coffee?

"Honestly, Carmine was a mistake from the very beginning. I should never have come to a small town. I should never have gotten a job at a cafe where so many people would be snooping around, asking questions."

"Guess you're referring to Peter Piatek of *The Carmine Enquirer*."

I threw up my hands. "Well, if you know everything already, why am I bothering to talk?"

Roberta took a sip of her coffee and grimaced. Then she nodded at the chair opposite hers.

"Sit."

I grabbed a can of ginger ale and sat down with a heavy sigh. My back spasmed as I sat, reminding me of the many hours spent at the police station.

"Here are the facts we've got to work with: Jay Casanova has attempted to uphold his image of innocence among his most die-hard followers. My initial fears were that a crazed fan would attack you. But Jay is in prison. He'll stay there for many years, possibly until the day he dies. His popularity is waning, and polls show that more and more people believe you spoke the truth in court."

"Well, that's nice."

"It appears Jay Casanova, increasingly, is no threat to you."

"Appears so?" I said, knowing it wasn't true. Otherwise, I wouldn't be in witness protection in a small town in New Jersey.

"Harry Casanova, his brother and business partner, has gone missing. The DEA struggled to connect him to Jay Casanova's crimes, but new evidence has come to light. Before they could bring him in for questioning, he disappeared. It's my belief he's looking for you."

"He wants to do what Jay can't do."

"That's right. He wants revenge on you for testifying against his brother and destroying their business empire. Since they indicted Jay Casanova on trafficking drugs and guns, Casanova Enterprises has filed for bankruptcy. Many of the brothers' assets have been seized as part of the DEA investigation. If Harry is indicted, too—which I believe he will be—he too will spend the rest of his life behind bars."

"But how does coming after me change any of that?"

"It doesn't. The man wants revenge, Bernie. It's not a rational thing."

"He's crazy."

Roberta nodded. "Crazy as a loon."

I took a sip of ginger ale, thinking through the implications. No matter how I looked at it, it was bad. And my situation in Carmine made it worse.

"All the more reason for me to leave this town, Roberta. It's only a matter of days before someone figures out who I am. The chief of police already knows and—"

"Chief Tedesco," she said. "I know. I told her."

"You what?"

I gaped at Roberta.

"The U.S. Marshalls Service can't protect you 24/7. So, as

per best practice, I informed the local chief of police, Diana Tedesco, so she knows about your situation. We're confident —I'm confident—that you're as safe here in Carmine as you could be."

My stomach tightened, threatening to curl up and play dead. I could see Roberta's logic. In theory, local cops keeping an eye out for me was safer than me solely relying on my own secrecy. But Chief Tedesco wanted to pin Mark's murder on me.

"Roberta, I don't think I'm so safe here in Carmine."

"The computer disagrees."

"The computer?"

Roberta reached down to the floor, where a laptop bag rested against her chair. She pulled out a slim laptop and opened it. She tapped a few keys and swiveled the device so I could see the screen.

A spreadsheet with seemingly endless columns of information.

"What is this?" I asked.

"Your witness protection matchmaking report. The computer, aided by artificial intelligence, analyzes a data set covering 399 factors, such as place of birth, parents' education, your favorite music in high school, and so on."

"My favorite music? You're saying that because I listened to punk music in high school, your computer chose Carmine as the best place for me to hide out?"

"Punk music, Bernie?" Roberta raised an eyebrow. "Are you being completely honest with yourself? This isn't the music you used as a social lubricant with friends. This is what genuinely sparked joy in you."

"Right—punk music," I insisted.

Roberta stared at me. I thought. I knew what my favorite music was, I'd always known it was punk, and I—

A memory flared into my mind. Fireplace with flames crackling. Eggnog. Wool blanket over my legs. I could almost hear the music playing on the stereo...

I stared at Roberta, amazed. She was right. My favorite music hadn't been punk.

"Christmas music," I said.

"Correct." Roberta swiped the mouse pad on her laptop, scrolling down and pointing out cell B273, C273, and D273. "Specifically, holiday songs by Frank Sinatra, Dean Martin, and Nat King Cole. Also, you have a soft spot for 'Dominick the Donkey.'"

She turned the laptop around again.

"The computer doesn't lie. Carmine is the best option for you. What you need to do is meet people, make friends, put down roots."

An echo of what Officer Ferrante had said in the car. I sighed. Was everyone out to get me killed? Couldn't they just leave me alone and let me hide away? I would go anywhere, as long as I could keep my secret.

I crossed my arms over my chest. "I won't stay, Roberta. I don't care what the computer says. Carmine isn't for me."

"You don't even know Carmine."

"I know enough about it," I said. "Now show me what the computer recommends as a Plan B. There is a Plan B, isn't there?"

Roberta sighed and shook her head. "Of course there is." She tapped on her keys and then swung the laptop around for me to see. "Here we go. The computer has one other option for you—just one—and this is it."

A PDF report was open on the screen. An image dominated the top. The photo showed a cabin surrounded by deep snow, the roof covered in a thick blanket of white.

Snow shoes hung on the wall next to the front door. In the background stood tall pine trees.

"What's this?" I said.

"This is Alaska."

A chill went through me. The place looked freezing cold. But I couldn't rule it out. I stared at the picture, trying hard to imagine living there. "I hear Anchorage is a big enough city. How close is this to Anchorage?"

"This is nowhere near Anchorage. In fact, Bernie, this is nowhere near anything. The computer concludes that if Carmine is still too big, too connected to keep you safe, we need to go more remote. And this—" She pointed to the photo. "— is as remote as it gets."

"It looks—"

I failed to find the right words. It looked lonesome. And cold. So cold.

"How chilly does it get?"

"Oh, 40 below is pretty common. Though it can hit 70 below in winter."

I shuddered. I thought of Los Angeles, waking up to sunshine nearly every day of the year. If the temperature dropped below 60 degrees, people would complain. "People" being me.

Speaking of people…

"How close is this cabin to its neighbors?"

"The closest neighbor is three miles."

My stomach shrank to the size of a tennis ball. I'd told myself I needed to get far away from people with all their questions. But the thought of living so far from other human beings made feel a little sick. I took another swig of ginger ale.

"I can't live there," I admitted.

"Fresh air, fishing, the Northern Lights—the place has a

lot going for it," Roberta said.

"I'm sure it does," I said. "And it would make someone very, very happy. Only that someone isn't me. Can you even get internet up there? TV? A decent cup of coffee? What's the nearest cafe? I would go crazy. I would—"

I would freeze to death.

I shook my head. "I can't do it."

Roberta stared at me, then shrugged. "Okey-dokey," she said. She closed the laptop, mercifully removing the cabin from view.

"Carmine is your only other option, Bernie."

"My only option..." I said in a daze.

Somehow I'd imagined Roberta would fix my problems, whisking me away from Carmine and Chief Tedesco and the unhappy mess I'd landed in.

"But I don't even have a job," I said.

As soon as I'd said it, I realized how important a detail that was. Even if I didn't go to Alaska, I needed, as the U.S. Marshalls Service defined it, "gainful employment." There had to be a Plan C.

"Carmine is small, and no one is hiring. I don't have a car and can't afford one, so even if the computer thinks it's a good personality match, I really don't think the logistics work out. Unless, of course, I could get a car and commute to, say, New York City. I'd stay in Carmine, but only to sleep. My daily life would be in the city. The big, anonymous city. There are lots of jobs in New York, and let's be honest, without a decent job, I'll never build a new life."

Roberta slid a postcard across the table. On the front was a photograph of a bakery. I recognized it even before I read the sign above the front door: Moroni's Italian Bakery.

"What's this?"

"Flip it over."

I turned the postcard. On the back, in smooth, curvaceous handwriting, it said:

Bernie—see you at 5 pm!
XO Angelica.

I looked up at Roberta. "What is this?"

"This," she said with a triumphant smile, "is an invitation to a job interview."

~

Inside, Moroni's Italian Bakery was warm in every sense of the word. The late afternoon sun cast a golden sheen across the tiled floor and the air was toasty and fragrant with the smells of baking cookies and freshly ground coffee.

Still, as I sat at one of the cafe tables, I shivered and wrapped my arms around myself. My body ached, and not just from the chair at the police station. I was bone-weary. It had been a long, hard day.

"This should help," Angelica said, placing a warm cup in my hands. My nose filled with the rich scent of chocolate.

"Hot chocolate?" I asked.

"A Moroni family secret. But trust me, it will make you feel better. Just checking: You're over 21, right?"

"You're flattering me," I mumbled.

"Where hot chocolate fails, flattery can work wonders."

I took a sip of the hot chocolate. It was sweet and strong, and its warmth spread from my chest out into every limb. I let out a long sigh.

"This is magic," I said.

Angelica's face lit up with a giant smile.

Even without the smile, she had a beautiful face. A long aquiline nose held up a pair of thick, black brows, perfectly complementing her chocolate-brown eyes. Her black hair, streaked on one side as if with a single white brushstroke, struggled to free itself from hairpins, and a curly strand hung loose down her cheek.

I finished the hot chocolate and before I could protest, she'd grabbed the mug and returned behind the counter to make another.

The glass counter ran all the way from the front door to the back, where another, smaller display case extended perpendicularly to the long one. Behind the glass lay a dizzying array of Italian baked goods: amaretti, pignoli and rainbow cookies, macaroons, and dozens of other kinds that I couldn't name.

A door at the back led to a hallway, and I assumed, the bakery.

Half a dozen small tables dominated the rest of the space, each decorated with a stocky candle in the tricolor of the Italian flag: red, white, and green.

Behind the counter, Angelica ducked down. I heard a cupboard open, and she came up with a bottle. I was pretty sure it was liquor—her secret ingredient—but I wasn't going to argue that it was too early for anything. After finding a dead body and being accused of murder, I was willing to rethink my rules around happy hour.

She came back to the table and handed me the cup of steaming hot chocolate. She sat down and watched me drink.

As the warmth spread through me, my limbs grew heavier and heavier. My shoulders slumped. My eyelids slid down. I blinked and sat up straight.

I bit my lip. Had Angelica noticed? I was supposed to be interviewing for a job and here I was falling asleep.

"You must be exhausted," she said and reached across the table, laying a hand on mine.

I nodded, at a loss for what to say. Her touch sent more warmth through my body, and I was suddenly aware of how long ago someone had comforted me.

Angelica's face blurred around the edges.

"Here, *mia cara*," she said, handing me a napkin.

I wiped the tears from my eyes.

"Sorry."

The door opened, and a bell jingled softly overhead, as delicate as a wind chime, and a customer came into the cafe.

Angelica got to her feet. "Want to give me a hand?"

I nodded and followed, my body feeling half asleep.

The customer ordered two dozen pignoli cookies and paid. Then he dawdled, obviously pretending to look at the display case, and every few seconds casting me a glance.

"Have a nice day, Victor," Angelica said.

It was clearly a nudge to get him to leave. He gave her a sheepish smile and cast me another curious glance before hurrying out the door. The next customer, an elderly woman with an unfortunate head of orange hair, stepped forward, ordering a dozen cannolis.

"Help me with these, will you?" Angelica asked me.

Hardly thinking, my mind in a muddle, I washed my hands at a sink by the back wall. She showed me where the cardboard boxes were and I put one together and carefully filled it with cannolis.

Meanwhile, Angelica dealt with the payment as yet another customer came in. This customer showed as much interest in me as in the sesame cookies she was ordering, her eyes scanning me ravenously.

"You're the talk of the town," Angelica whispered to me as, together, we filled a bag with the cookies.

I groaned. "Oh, no. That's the last thing I want."

"Don't worry, sweetie. It'll blow over. They'll find whoever did this horrible thing and then it will become another piece of gossip. Carmine has lots of gossip. If you have nothing shocking to add to the story, then your part won't matter so much."

Would my secret identity as the actress who played Eve Silver, now hiding in witness protection, qualify as "shocking"? I was pretty sure it would.

Angelica's brow furrowed. "As long as Chief Tedesco doesn't do something silly, of course."

"What do you mean, silly?"

My stomach did a three-quarter turn, making me queasy.

"Well, earlier today, Chief Tedesco stopped by to ask me some questions. Diana has always been even-keeled. Although after what her sister did to her..."

"What did her sister do to her?"

Angelica sighed. "Diana was happily married and loved her husband. But there was one person she loved even more. Her sister. They weren't just sisters, they were best friends. Until..."

"What? What happened?"

"I shouldn't gossip."

"Please, Angelica. I won't tell anyone."

"Diana's husband had an affair and Diana caught him in the act."

I put a hand to my mouth. "No. Not the sister."

Angelica nodded. "That was last month, and Chief Tedesco has been acting strange ever since. But can you blame her?"

I felt sympathy for Diana Tedesco. What a blow it must have been to her to discover that her best friend—her own sister—was having an affair with her husband.

"Still, *maronna mia*," Angelica continued, "today Chief Tedesco was so worked up. I expected her to say she'd caught you red-handed stabbing Mark in the back. See, she said the security camera outside Joanna's offices—that's Joanna Parisi of Parisi & Parisi—it shows no one near the cafe, except Mark and then you."

"The killer must have come in the back," I said.

"And Diana did say that. She said the person must have had a key. Which employees do."

"Employees like me," I said, my stomach turning again. I swallowed the nausea with a gulp. "I think only Mark and I had keys to the cafe."

"There must be a perfectly reasonable explanation," Angelica quickly said. "And Diana herself admitted she had no tangible leads yet."

I could almost hear Chief Tedesco's cool voice emphasize that last word: "Yet."

How would I view the crime scene if I were the cop? I put myself in Chief Tedesco's shoes. Or tried to. Somehow I pictured her shoes one size too small, squeezing my toes and making me grumpy. Maybe her heart was a couple of sizes too small, too.

I put myself in Eve Silver's shoes instead. That was a better fit. How would she—detective extraordinaire—approach this investigation?

First, she'd say the motive was too thin. The suspect didn't stand to gain by killing her boss and bringing more attention to herself.

Thank you, Eve. My thoughts exactly.

Next, what was the concrete evidence? There was only one suspect, and everything pointed to her guilt.

They had caught her fleeing the scene of the crime (once again, I inwardly groaned at my stupid decision to run). Apart from the obvious—Mark's body with a knife in his back—there were no indications anyone else had been present at the cafe that morning.

I sighed. So much for Eve Silver solving the case.

With a smile, Angelica handed the bag of sesame cookies to the customer.

"An espresso, please," a man said.

Angelica turned to me, an eyebrow raised, silently asking me if I wanted to make the coffee. I hurried to the espresso machine. It was long and gleaming. If the one at Cafe Roma had been a rusty old scrapheap, this was a sports car. I made the espresso, inhaling the rich scent of coffee as it poured into the little cup. Even the coffee smelled ten times better here than at Cafe Roma.

I placed the cup with its little saucer on the counter, and the man thanked me. He downed his espresso with expert grace. At the same time, his phone rang. He fumbled for his phone and set the cup down, missing the saucer and placing it on the glass counter instead.

He walked away, talking into his phone.

Angelica removed the cup and saucer and tossed me a cloth to wipe off the counter. The espresso cup had left a round smudge.

I froze, my hand holding the cloth over the smudge. An image flashed across my mind. I saw Cafe Roma again and the counter with Mark's keys and the paperback lying next to his half-finished cappuccino. And something else, too.

There had been a smudge next to Mark's cup, and now I

knew what it was. It was a coffee ring. But a small one. Not the size of a regular coffee cup. An espresso cup.

When Mark and I had closed the cafe for the day, I had wiped that counter.

It was unlikely that Mark, the morning he died, had made an espresso, drunk it, then removed the cup before making himself a cappuccino. No, someone else had drunk that espresso and removed the cup afterward. The killer.

Angelica was eyeing me with apparent concern, her head cocked to the side.

"Your thoughts are far away," she said.

"I'm sorry," I said. "My mind is on the job."

I was in no state to do a job interview. If I were Angelica, I wouldn't hire me.

"Try this, Bernie."

She leaned into the counter, and retrieving a cookie, handed it to me.

Only it wasn't a cookie. It was a handful of marble-sized balls of fried dough, sticky with honey, and covered in colorful sprinkles.

I popped them in my mouth. The fried dough and honey melted on my tongue, the sprinkles adding a little crunch between my teeth, and I closed my eyes for a moment, savoring the incredible flavor.

"It's *struffoli*," Angelica said.

"Wow," I said, and my stomach rumbled in agreement.

I put a hand on my gut, embarrassed by the sound.

Angelica let out a huff of exasperation. "Angelica, you fool. This poor woman is suffering from starvation and you've got her running around the bakery serving people. When was the last time you ate, Bernie?"

"This morning at breakfast," I said. But I was quick to

add: "But it's fine, I'll find some food after this. I've got frozen pizza at home."

"No, no, no." Angelica waved her hands. "Out of the question. You will eat and you will eat well. Maybe we can get Carlo—he's my brother and owns the restaurant next door—to bring over a plate of lasagna…"

"Don't worry about it, Angelica," a voice said.

Nat stood on the other side of the counter. I hadn't even noticed that he'd entered as the last customer had left. He smiled and pushed his glasses back on his nose.

"Bernie won't need food from Carlo's."

"I won't?"

"Nope. Because you're coming with me to the Old Mill for a drink and a bite to eat."

I backed away from the counter and put up my hands. "Uh, no thanks—I've got plans…"

Suddenly, the lights in Moroni's felt too bright. A person passing outside on the sidewalk looked in, gazing at me with obvious curiosity. I couldn't risk going to the Old Mill with Nat, let alone work at Moroni's, which had a constant stream of customers.

But Angelica clapped her hands together with delight.

"Great idea, Nat. But don't keep her out too late, you hear?" She turned to me and put a gentle hand on my cheek. "You need to get some rest, Bernie, so you're ready for your first day of work tomorrow morning."

My face felt hot. Should I be happy or horrified?

"I can't," I spluttered. "I shouldn't…"

Angelica smiled. "Oh, you'll do great."

∼

As Nat held open the door to the Old Mill, I made a promise to myself: I would stay for a bite to eat and one drink. Be a wallflower. Then be gone. I could still catch a few episodes of *Murder, She Wrote* before bedtime.

"You coming?" he said.

I sighed and stepped inside.

The Old Mill was a long, low wooden structure, and it was easy to see that it had once been a sawmill, as Nat had informed me on the ride over. Exposed wooden beams cut across the ceiling. Wide floorboards stretched under the few tables and booths. The long bar gleamed with the confidence of polished hardwood.

"Welcome to Carmine's best bar," Nat said. "It's also our only bar. But if you must have just one bar, the Old Mill ain't bad."

A stuffed deer head jutted out of a wall, antlers and all, and below it stood an old jukebox. The music piped out of top-notch speakers placed high in the dark corners of the ceiling was pure throwback: "Mack the Knife" by Bobby Darin. It would have felt old school if the bartender didn't sport a beard and a flannel shirt that would have been at home in Portland, Oregon.

"This is Jerry," Nat said, introducing me to the bearded bartender.

He gave a small nod. "Drink?" he asked, apparently a man of few words.

"Beer, please."

He pointed at the taps built into the bar.

I pointed at one of the craft brews.

He nodded, grabbed a pint glass, and pressed down the tap handle to fill it.

Something about his demeanor eased the tension in my chest. Here was a guy I could sit across from at the bar, and drink after drink, he wouldn't ask me questions, instead offering companionable silence.

If only the rest of Carmine's citizens were as tight-lipped.

Nat ordered a beer as well, and when we each had our pint glasses in hand, we raised them.

"Here's to good coffee," Nat said.

"And freshly made cannolis," I added.

We drank. The beer was delicious. Dry and crisp with a sharp hoppy bitterness. Maybe I should swap my ginger ale for some beer at home.

"Quiet tonight," Nat said. "But not bad for a weeknight."

There were probably half a dozen people in the place, besides Nat and myself. I recognized the woman who'd quarreled with Mark. She was a classic beauty, with brown curls and full red lips. I wondered what the connection was between her and Mark. She was sitting in a booth talking to two other women, both younger.

Nat caught me looking and said, "That's Maria Ferrante. The one with short red hair is Emma Francis."

The red-head, Emma, was leaning close to the other two women, listening rapturously to what Maria had to say. From where we stood, I had a good view of her face. Freckled cheeks, with a roundness that I suspected would vanish in a year or two as adulthood squeezed out the last of her "baby fat."

"Emma's aunt and uncle live on Cedar Hill," Nat continued. "That's the fancy part of town. After graduating from college, she came to stay with them. She worked at Moroni's over the summer to make some extra cash. She's starting graduate school in a few weeks. Masters in Psychology."

Emma caught sight of us and beamed, waving at Nat. He waved back.

"Friendly," I remarked. "Who's that next to her, in the corner? The blonde."

"That's Susan Davis. She works at Joanna Parisi's law firm."

"Parisi & Parisi?"

"That's the one. The other Parisi is her husband, Gino."

The name "Susan" was ringing a bell.

"Did you tell me about a Susan at some point?" I asked Nat.

He nodded. "I did. She's another veteran from Cafe Roma. She's Mark's cousin."

"The one he fired?"

Nat grinned. "That's the one."

He pointed out a group of guys sitting in another booth. Among them was a dark, handsome guy I recognized.

"Isn't that Officer Ferrante?" I asked, trying to sound casual about it.

"Anthony Ferrante," Nat said. "Good-looking, isn't he?"

"Ferrante? Maria's husband, I guess."

My heart sank a little. Of course, Officer Ferrante was married. But why was I even thinking about good-looking guys? I couldn't afford the luxury of dating, not when I was actively trying to stay hidden.

"Brother and sister," Nat said.

My heart did its annoying fluttery thing again.

Carmine can't be a long-term solution, I told my heart. *So forget about it.*

I wondered if Chief Tedesco had shared the intel on me, revealing my true identity to her officers. It made me feel strangely unsettled to think Officer Ferrante, cop pinup of the month, had been briefed about me.

Uh, Earth to Bernie, hello? Remember your promise. One drink. Wallflower. Then home. Got it?

Got it.

As Nat and I were speaking, Emma got up from her seat to allow Susan out of the booth.

Susan came to the bar and Nat introduced us.

"Where are you from?" she asked me.

A simple and very reasonable question, but it made my heart hammer wildly.

"California," I said. Then almost gasped. That wasn't my line. I was supposed to say "out west" or "Michigan."

"Michigan, actually," I said. "Michigan."

"Where in California did you live?" Susan said, ignoring my mention of Michigan. "I'm going to California."

"Susan's big dream is to go into showbiz," Nat explained.

"Not just a dream," Susan said, giving Nat a playful push. "I'm going. In fact, I almost have enough savings to make it happen. This fall I'm going to move to L.A. and enroll in the Casanova Acting Academy. Or whatever it's called now." She put a hand over her heart. "What a shock that they wrongfully accused Jay—and then that they actually sentenced him to prison."

I gripped my pint glass hard, hoping it was strong enough and wouldn't shatter in my white-knuckled hands. I took a sip of beer to hide my reaction. Just my luck to meet an aspiring actress who was a Jay Casanova fan. Had Roberta's genius computer included data on Susan Davis? Because this wasn't ideal.

Susan was rattling off details about why the academy was so fantastic.

As she talked, I studied her. A hint of dark roots by her scalp revealed she dyed her hair blonde. With her high cheekbones and blue eyes, plus the platinum blonde bangs, she fit the model of a Gold Girl to a tee.

That was the name the media had given the actresses

that Jay Casanova liked to pair up with for his role as Adam Gold in the spinoff movies. The prototype had been Eve Silver—me—in the show *Silver & Gold*. For Jay's feature length movies, he'd chosen a new female co-star each time. Adam Gold always played opposite a blonde with bangs, and he demanded that women dye their hair the exact color he wanted. In fact, these days you could go to any stylist in America and say, "I want a Gold Girl hairdo," and they'd know exactly what you wanted.

Susan flicked a blonde curl over her shoulders and explained why the acting curriculum wasn't the most important reason she'd chosen the Casanova Acting Academy.

"The industry's all about who you know, and the academy helps you make connections," Susan explained to me. "Hard work and talent aren't enough."

As she lectured me on how Hollywood worked and what the life of an actress looked like, I relaxed a little. She assumed I was entirely ignorant of what happened in show biz. Which meant she had no suspicions about my true identity. Good. All I had to do was listen and nod and pretend to be interested, and keep feigning ignorance.

Susan ordered a round of drinks "for the girls" and then headed back to the booth where Emma and Maria were sitting.

"She's got big ambitions," Nat commented after she was out of earshot. "Ever since she played the lead in the high school musical, she's been unbearable. Can you imagine what a pain she'll be if she actually becomes famous?"

"Is she a talented actress?" I asked.

"Does it matter? She's got the look."

It was a cynical opinion, but clearly he'd seen what I'd seen: She had potential as a Gold Girl. Yet, in my experience, the ones who had "the look," but couldn't struggle their way through a script, didn't last long. Studio executives loved a pretty face, but there were so many to choose from—why not pick one that could also act?

Anyway, I didn't have to worry about that anymore. My acting career was over, with only the happy memories of playing Eve Silver left.

I took another gulp of beer, emptying my glass.

There are no return tickets to the past, I told myself. *It's time to move on.*

In fact, it was time to go home.

I slipped off my stool and turned to Nat, preparing to say goodnight, when he brought up a bag and pulled out cylindrical packages in butcher paper.

"What's this?"

"Subs from Martini's Italian Market. I told you we were eating dinner. The Old Mill doesn't serve food, but we can bring in takeout."

Nat waved a hand, and from down the bar, Jerry responded with a grunt. Before I could stop him, he poured another couple of pints of beer.

"Let's eat," Nat said.

I settled back onto the bar stool with a sigh, mentally revising my promise to myself: I'd have a bite to eat and one more drink, no more, then I'd go home.

One more drink, Bernie. No more.

4

Despite wearing sunglasses, I had to squint against the Wednesday morning glare. The sun seemed to have cranked up the light to eleven, and it made my head pound.

The little bell over the front door jingled as I entered Moroni's, and I winced—its delicate chime sounded like the bells of Notre Dame clashing in my head.

Angelica smiled. She was standing by a cafe table, on which sat a plate with a pastry and a steaming cup of coffee.

"Nat sent me a message last night spilling your secret."

I froze in the doorway. What had I told Nat last night? I tried to remember, recalling one pint of beer after another, coins fed into the jukebox, arms slung around Nat's shoulders as we crooned to an old Sinatra song.

I groaned, and not just because my head hurt. Had I made more of a fool of myself than I remembered? Had I told him who I was?

"That's right, young lady," Angelica said teasingly. "I know all about your hangover. Now come sit."

Apparently, she would not accuse me of being the

famous actress Bernadette Kovac. I relaxed and shuffled over to the table.

"What's this?"

"*Maritozzi*, it's called," Angelica explained. "It's popular in Rome and originally was the traditional sweetbread eaten at Lent. Now, thankfully, we can eat it whenever we want. It's good for a hangover."

I sat down, unsure whether the cream-filled bun was a good idea. My stomach felt askew. I started with a sip of coffee, which was so strong, my eyes watered.

Then I tried the pastry. It was nothing like any other breakfast I'd ever had. A sweet bun with pine nuts and raisins, and a little candied orange peel, which was then cut open and filled with rich, homemade whipped cream. It looked impossibly decadent, but as I ate it, I found it not only sweet, but filling.

Angelica made herself a coffee and joined me again at the table. She sipped it as I devoured my delicious maritozzi bun. Remarkably, I felt more human already.

"So, what's the plan for today? Will it be a busy day?"

Angelica made an impatient gesture. "Busy? That's not the word. We'll be swamped. You know, I had help over the summer. Emma Francis—have you met her?—she was working here, but she stopped. She's off to graduate school after Labor Day." Angelica shook her head. "Before she came along, I told myself I was fine. I could handle the bakery by myself, and when things got extra busy, I could ask my brother, Carlo, for a helping hand. But I was wrong. There's a lot we can do alone, but to face life—with all its joys and its difficulties—you need a helping hand. And sometimes the hardest part of facing a challenge is asking for that help. Having Emma work for me taught me that. So, with

Carmine's annual street festival coming up, not to mention the big cannoli competition, I'll need all the help I can get."

I nodded as I took another bite of the maritozzi. This all sounded wise—clearly, Angelica had learned an important lesson.

"So," she said, putting down her cup with a decisive clink. "I'm asking: Are you ready to help?"

～

AT MIDDAY, Angelica dismissed me, telling me to take a long lunch and insisting she didn't want to run me ragged on my first day. When I protested that the work was helping me forget all the bad things that had happened, she shook her head.

"You come to Moroni's not to forget, but to remember."

I gave her a puzzled look, and she smiled and patted my hand. "You'll understand when you understand."

I stepped out of the bakery with a lightness in my step that I hadn't felt in a long while. My hangover was gone, and the aches I felt in my back and arms were from good, hard work in the bakery—kneading dough and mixing ingredients and carrying trays of baked cookies from the ovens to the counter in the cafe.

My light step faltered as I caught sight of Cafe Roma across the street. I stopped. The cafe's shutters were raised all the way. The windows were dark, the front entrance blocked by crime scene tape. A cluster of people stood on the corner of Poplar and Garibaldi, talking and gesturing at the cafe.

Before they could see me, I hurried down Garibaldi Avenue. I strode past Carlo's Restaurant, Russo's Realty,

Milano Books, and other storefronts before I came to Martini's Italian Market.

Inside, I headed straight for the deli and ordered an Italian sub with mortadella and provolone. I got them to wrap it and headed for the fridges at the back to pick out a soda. For a moment, my hand hovered over a ginger ale. Then I remembered my sad fridge at home and chose a bottle of iced tea instead.

Outside, I looked around for a place to sit. Beyond Martini's, a park stretched across a long town block. A sign at the entrance said, "Puccini Park." I found a bench under a stand of sycamores and ate my lunch.

Last night had been a mistake, I reflected. Nat was nice and all, but I shouldn't have gotten carried away and—

And had fun?

I sighed. The truth was that Nat and I had a blast at the Old Mill. I'd laughed. I'd felt happy.

If I was honest with myself—and I had to remember Roberta's little lesson about honesty (Christmas music, not punk music)—I was already looking forward to another night at the Old Mill with Nat.

But could I risk another night of fun?

My mind was in a muddle, and it had nothing to do with the hangover. I finished my sub and iced tea and threw the wrapping paper and bottle in a nearby garbage can. Then I took a walk to clear my head. A car slowly circled the park, but I took no notice. I needed to put my thoughts in order.

I left the park and crossed Garibaldi Avenue and turned down a side street.

Rimini Street led to another tree-lined neighborhood. The ranch-style homes here were more modest than my own. Lawns ran wild, kids' toys lay strewn across cracked driveways, and plywood covered the windows of one house I passed. Behind Garibaldi Avenue's manicured facade, Carmine had an unhappy side, too.

My thoughts returned to Mark Lewis and the crime scene. The killer must have come in the back using keys...

Or did he?

The smudge from an espresso cup. Mark's keys on the counter. Back door locked. Front door, too. The sound of a door slamming.

An idea was forming in my mind...

Occasionally, a kid raced by me on a bike, or a car rumbled past, but otherwise, it was quiet. Most people were at work. Which was why it didn't take me long to notice that I was being followed.

The car kept its distance. Still, I could hear its engine, the steadiness of its rumbling as it drifted behind me, and then when I turned off Rimini Street onto St. Francis Avenue, I saw it.

It was a police cruiser.

That should have reassured me, I suppose, since it wasn't a madman with a shotgun stalking me. No, it was the Carmine police shadowing me. This was no doubt Chief Tedesco's doing. She was keeping an eye on me.

I clenched my fists and increased my stride. I marched onto Modena Street. There was no sidewalk, so I walked on the cracked and potholed blacktop alongside the curb. I could sense the car speeding up to keep pace with me.

At the end of the street, I turned right onto Cabrini Avenue. There was a low tree on the corner, and together with a hedge, it blocked the view from Modena Street.

As soon as I'd rounded the corner, I stopped and crouched down, making sure the driver of the car wouldn't be able to see me.

The car reached the end of Modena Street and idled. No

doubt the driver was craning his neck to see where I went, and although the windows were down, I couldn't see who drove the car.

I jumped out of my hiding place and up to the car window.

Behind the wheel sat Officer Anthony Ferrante.

"Jeez," he said. "Was I that obvious?"

"Why are you following me?"

He turned away, his hands gripping the steering wheel as he refused to meet my eyes.

"I'm supposed to keep an eye on you," he said. "Chief's orders."

"I see." I would have enjoyed staring at his handsome face, if it weren't for the anger that was coursing through me like electricity. "You think I'd kill my boss because we disagreed about a cannoli?"

He shook his head. Then bravely turned his attention back to me. "Look, I don't like this detail. Honestly. But Chief Tedesco—"

"Chief Tedesco and I need to talk," I said, shocking myself as much as I apparently shocked Officer Ferrante. He flexed his fingers on the wheel, clearly nervous.

As soon as I'd said the words, I knew I was right. Chief Tedesco represented justice in this town. She knew about my placement in witness protection and how precarious my situation in Carmine was. If she was a serious officer of the law, she would want to find the right killer, not nail the murder on the first fool who walked in on the dead body. I refused to play the patsy.

"Take me down to the station," I demanded. "I want to speak to Chief Tedesco now."

"She's not at the station. She went home for lunch."

"Then take me to her house."

Officer Ferrante gazed at me, probably thinking I was crazy. Then he sighed and leaned over and opened the passenger door.

"All right," he said. "Hop in."

~

Chief of Police Diana Tedesco lived at the far end of Verdi Lane, a few streets from my own home. I had pictured her living in something big and solid, like a Scottish castle, complete with dungeons and torture chambers. But of course they didn't have those in Carmine.

In fact, her house was a modest ranch with ivy-covered trellises and a well-kept lawn.

Officer Ferrante didn't accompany me to the door. Maybe he was one of those guys who would happily take a bullet to protect and serve, yet cowered under the couch whenever two women had a confrontation.

I rang the doorbell, which chimed inside. Distantly, I could hear a TV or radio. Then steps came toward me. The door opened.

Chief Tedesco's eyes widened. She took a step backward.

But then recovered quickly.

She frowned. "What do you want, Miss Smyth?"

Was it my imagination of did she say my name—my assumed name—with sarcasm? She gazed over my shoulder toward Officer Ferrante, which only deepened her frown.

"I'd like to talk to you about the murder of Mark Lewis," I said. "Can I come in?"

She pushed the door, halfway closing it. "You can tell me what you need to tell me right here."

I sighed. She wasn't going to make this easy. Behind her, TV voices fought for my attention. I could glimpse the corner of a framed print on the hallway wall and a little table with a ceramic bowl for keys and coins.

"My only crimes are finding Mark and then panicking," I said. "Although you seem to suspect me, I had no reason to kill him. You know how important a new life in Carmine is to me. I needed that job badly. I may not have liked him, but that's no reason to kill someone."

"Interesting that you should say that," Chief Tedesco said with a bitterness that surprised me.

I tried another tack. "Look, I remembered something. It may be important. There was a coffee ring on the counter. I noticed it when I found Mark, and it was only later that I realized why it stood out."

I explained my theory about the espresso cup, and how it suggested Mark had a visitor before me. "The killer was there when I arrived. I'm almost sure of it. I heard a door slam. It must have been the door between the cafe and the kitchen—or else the back door. The killer locked the back door. Why bother? Well, to slow me down and allow the fire to take hold."

Chief Tedesco said nothing, simply continuing to glare at me. It wasn't a good sign, but it wasn't a bad sign, either. At least I still had her attention.

"So, based on clues, who could the killer be? As far as we know, only two people had keys. Mark and myself. So Mark must have let the killer into the cafe. If the killer had been any old stranger, he probably wouldn't have let them in. Even if he did, would he then have offered them an espresso? Mark was notoriously cheap. There would be a sales record for the espresso. But I bet there isn't."

"There isn't," Chief Tedesco confirmed.

"Right," I said, excited to see an opportunity to find common ground with the chief. "Which means that he did give the visitor an espresso for free. It would have to be someone close to him or he'd demand money."

"Or, Miss Smyth, he'd simply dock their pay." She narrowed her eyes. "An employee could make the espresso and then Mark would have subtracted it from her paycheck. An employee knew when Mark would be at work and when others were likely to turn up. She had the keys to get in and out. She knew where the knife was."

"But she wouldn't gain anything from killing her boss, least of all if her greatest desire was to keep a low profile," I protested. "Look, you have to believe me…"

Behind Chief Tedesco, the voices on the TV argued about something. It was as if they were echoing our conversation, as if one of them was me, demanding to be heard.

My whole body tensed as it dawned on me: There was a reason I thought the TV sounded like me. Because it was me. The voice coming from the TV within the house was Eve Silver.

"*Mr. Henslow's body was found in the lake,*" Eve Silver was saying on the TV. "*But the autopsy showed he'd swallowed saltwater.*"

"*He didn't drown in the boating accident.*" (That was Adam Gold, Jay Casanova, my former co-star.)

"*Right. He was drowned in the ocean. Then the killer stuffed him in the trunk of his car and drove him to the lake and dumped him.*"

Both Chief Tedesco and I had gone quiet. I was listening intently. So was she. We were staring at each other, and a cold, horrible realization crept over me.

"We're done," she blurted. "You want to talk? Fine. Come to the station."

She swung the door shut. Slam. The lock clicked.

I stood on the front steps of Chief Tedesco's house,

dazed. As I turned around, I caught sight of Officer Ferrante in the cruiser. He was looking as uncomfortable as ever, entirely focused on the view of the street ahead. You'd think he was studying a particularly gnarly traffic jam, or he'd spotted several would-be burglars creeping around houses. But apart from a sprinkler spraying a neighbor's lawn, Verdi Lane was dead quiet.

Chief Tedesco, home for lunch, had been watching *Silver & Gold* when I interrupted her. If she'd been listening to NPR or WFUV or watching the Weather Channel, I wouldn't have given it a second thought. But *Silver & Gold* was old news. Either the rerun on TV was a massive coincidence or else Chief Tedesco had deliberately chosen to stream it during her lunch break.

Well, which was it?

And if she was deliberately watching *Silver & Gold*, was it because she was researching my background? Presumably she had a big case file from U.S. Marshall Roberta LaRosa. Watching Eve Silver solve mysteries with her dashing co-star could hardly constitute serious law enforcement research. Or could it?

I was halfway down the driveway, thinking I'd let Ferrante drive me home, when I decided I had to know. I swiveled around and cast a glance at the front windows. The lace curtains were undisturbed. There was no sign that Chief Tedesco was peeking out. I headed around the house.

Behind me, I heard Ferrante hiss at me, "Hey, Smyth, what do you think you're doing?"

But I kept going.

Around the side of the house, I found another window. The curtains were parted, providing an ample view of Chief Tedesco's modest kitchen-living room combo. Diana Tedesco sat at her kitchen bar, staring at a flatscreen TV mounted on the wall while eating pasta from a bowl. Leftovers? No, a discarded bag on the counter suggested a frozen, ready-made pasta meal. Which, no doubt, she'd microwaved. I had a moment to wonder at the sad state of her culinary experiences when those thoughts were interrupted.

No, not just interrupted. Blown apart.

Because not only did I see my own face on the TV screen—I was Eve Silver standing next to Jay Casanova as Adam Gold—I also saw Jay's face everywhere else in the living room. There were movie posters from all his feature films: *24-Karat Gold I, 24-Karat Gold II, The Adam Gold Files,* and *From Cold Case to Gold Case*. Plus framed photographic prints, one of Jay at the Academy Awards, grinning at the camera, one arm around his brother's shoulders. The print was signed. I recognized Jay's handwriting. The other scrawl was no doubt Harry's. There was also a heart-shaped pillow on the couch with Jay's face embroidered onto it. It looked distinctly homemade.

My hands had gone ice cold. I clenched them. Then unclenched them. This was beyond my worst nightmares.

Because everywhere I looked, there was irrefutable evidence: Chief Diana Tedesco was a die-hard Jay Casanova fan.

5

I strode down the street, walking so fast that I nearly broke into a run. My thoughts were dashing ahead of me, and no matter how much I quickened my pace, when I caught up with an idea, another would break away, and I'd chase that one instead.

Where was I going? Trees. Lawns. Driveways. The world was a rolling backdrop that meant nothing. The only image in my mind was Chief Tedesco's living room.

Lots of people enjoyed rewatching *Silver & Gold*. But what I'd seen through that window made my palms break into a cold sweat. The woman in charge of Mark's murder investigation apparently had a profound love for Jay Casanova, the man I had put in prison.

And what if she somehow equated the breakup of Eve Silver and Adam Gold with her own marriage?

I remembered what Roberta had told me: "...more and more people believe you spoke the truth in court." That meant some still believed that I had lied. Some still believed Jay Casanova was wrongfully convicted.

What if Chief Tedesco was among the people who saw

me as a villain? A traitor? Then I could kiss goodbye to any hope of clearing my name. I'd be better off leaving town, and leaving ASAP.

I dug my phone out of my pocket and stared at it. I could call Roberta and explain the situation, and she'd turn up in that mail truck and whisk me away.

Far, far away to Alaska.

And I'd spend my dying days in a snow-bound cabin, playing solitaire, unless I died before old age from frostbite or a polar bear attack.

Was I being melodramatic? Hey, even Eve Silver wouldn't survive long in the wilderness. In the *Silver & Gold* episode "The Moosehead Murders" (season 5, episode 7), Eve's city slicker smarts faced a serious antagonist: Mother Nature. In the end, Eve caught the killer, but not before Mamma Nature humiliated her.

I put away my phone. Leaving was out of the question. I had to make Carmine work.

But what could I do if the chief of police belonged to the sizable group of people who saw me as a backstabbing liar? She'd be on my back every hour of every day until she managed to pin the murder on me.

I kept walking.

As I turned a corner, I saw Garibaldi Avenue up ahead. It brought me back to reality and the sound of the car behind me. Officer Ferrante was still following me.

I spun around. He hit the brakes.

"You." I let my anger out at him, calling him several names that might have constituted assaulting an officer. "Can't you leave me alone?"

He opened the door on the driver's side and got out.

Leaning against the roof of the car, he shook his head. Slowly, sadly.

"Look, I'm sorry, Miss Smyth. I don't like this any more than you, but I can't ignore orders. I've got to stay close to you."

"So, what? You're going to trundle after me all day as I walk the mean streets of Carmine?"

Officer Ferrante frowned, thinking. Then he rubbed his chin.

"Well, there is another way—a way to make this less unpleasant..."

I crossed my arms. "Right. And what would that be?"

"You're new to town. I bet you haven't seen much more than Garibaldi Avenue. It seems to me you've stuck to home and work and not much else, and haven't taken in the sights."

"How would you know that?"

Ferrante colored. "Uh, well, Nat told me."

"Great. A snitch. Anything else he told you?"

"You haven't even seen the lake or the woods."

At the Old Mill Bar, Nat had grilled me about where I'd been, what had I seen in town since I arrived. Every negative answer got me a head shake and a tsk-tsk and a shame-on-you.

"So here's what I was thinking," he said, answering my question. "My boss says stick close to you. And you haven't seen half of Carmine. Well, why don't I give you the grand tour from the comfort of my cruiser so you can get to know your new home?"

"And you can keep an eye on me?"

He shrugged. "I'd rather play tour guide than follow you around like a spy."

I glared at him. It was sorely tempted to tell him where he could stick his tour. But his expression was so earnest, it was difficult to stay angry with him.

I took a deep breath and exhaled.

Plus, the more I thought about it, the more I appreciated the offer. Officer Ferrante had done me no wrong. His motive might be to keep tabs on me, but maybe I also had an ulterior motive. Maybe by getting friendly with Officer Ferrante, I was maintaining a connection to the police department, making sure I had a friend on the inside.

"All right," I said. "Show me this beautiful town of yours."

Ferrante grinned, and there was so much boyish charm in that smile that it melted the last of my anger. I couldn't help but smile.

"Where to first, Officer Ferrante?" I asked.

"Jump in," he said. "And please, call me Anthony."

I studied him for a moment. He was being friendly, that was all. Not sneaky. I had the feeling Anthony Ferrante didn't have a sneaky bone in his body. I made a decision: If he was going to be friendly, I would too.

"All right, Anthony. Call me Bernie."

"I will," he said and smiled. "Bernie."

∽

WE DROVE THROUGH TOWN, up Lake Road, and past the Old Mill, and Anthony explained how the original sawmill had been closed down after World War II, wiping out much of the town's economy.

"It's only in the past thirty years that Carmine has become more affluent again, and that's thanks to tourism."

Taking a sharp turn, he drove us back to town and then up a street that rose steeply uphill. Old trees lined the street. Large houses sat far back from the road, surrounded by wide lawns and beautifully manicured hedges and rose bushes.

"Cedar Hill," Anthony explained.

"Judging by the massive old Victorians, this must be where the rich live."

He nodded. "Cedar Hill has always been Carmine's fancy neighborhood."

We passed a large blue Victorian with two SUVs parked in the driveway. A yellow bicycle leaned against the garage.

The street crested the hill and then merged with a road that ran through the woods.

"We're back on Lake Road," Anthony explained. "Back there is the Old Mill. And over there is Old Quarry Road. But let's leave the quarry for another time. The lake is the real highlight."

Soon, the road twisted and swerved, and it became clear we'd left town. Occasionally I caught the glimpse of a house among the trees, but the farther along we went, the more wooded it became.

"It's beautiful out here," I said, meaning it.

"City people don't think of New Jersey as being green. They think of I-95 around Elizabeth, all concrete and fumes, and they forget about the rest of the state—we've got picture-perfect farmland and forests and hiking trails."

"Do you work for the police department or the tourism office?" I joked.

He laughed. "Guilty as charged. And just wait until you see the lake. Then I'll turn into a nature poet."

He steered onto an unpaved road, and the bumped over potholes as it entered a gravel parking lot. Ahead of us lay an old, wooden boathouse with a dock. A sandy beach stretched out next to it.

I got out of the car, and Anthony did, too.

The afternoon light twinkled on the waters of the lake, drawing lines of gold across its surface. Beyond the boathouse and the sand, large boulders, half-submerged in water, marked the edges of the lake. A hundred yards along, a tree leaned out from the woods, offering a comfortable seat for a fisherman, who smoked a pipe while he waited patiently for a tug on his line.

I could see why Anthony had said the lake would turn him into a nature poet. It was exquisite. I couldn't believe it looked so untouched.

"It's state land," he explained. "Though you'll find some houses tucked away in the woods, they're all leased. No one can own property on the lake. And motorboats are prohibited. So you'll only see rowboats, canoes, and kayaks, and the occasional electric outboard motor. Come on, let me show you the boathouse."

The red boathouse, a wide wooden structure, jutted out into the lake. Stepping inside, we entered a high-ceilinged, dark space. To either side stood racks with kayaks and canoes, chained and padlocked to keep thieves away. Anthony explained that some people kept their watercraft at home—outside of books I'd never heard anyone use the term "watercraft"—but those who didn't have the luxury of a big enough garage, he explained, could rent a space in the boathouse.

"That red kayak is Mark's," he said, pointing out one of the overturned vessels. "Kayaking was one of his few pastimes. When he wasn't at the cafe, he was out on the lake."

I didn't comment. The mention of Mark while standing in the boathouse brought back the memory of shooting a scene for *Silver & Gold* in a similar setting. In fact, the very episode Chief Tedesco had been watching.

In the original script for that episode, the killer lured Adam Gold into the boathouse and tried to stab him in the back. Eve Silver came to the rescue by grabbing an oar and throwing it at the killer like a spear, felling him.

But as we rehearsed the scene, Jay didn't like it. He insisted I couldn't save him. Adam should be the one to save Eve, he said, and threatened to cause problems if they didn't rewrite the scene at once. The director conceded. Who would want to defy America's heartthrob? So the writers reworked it and we reshot the scene. Eve never got to rescue Adam. Instead, it was Eve who nearly got knifed.

I half expected to see Jay Casanova's face emerge from the darkness. I shivered and rubbed my bare arms. Despite the warm day, it felt cool and damp in the boathouse.

Straight ahead, the boathouse opened a dock, reaching out into the water.

I hurried outside, glad to be in the fresh air again. Anthony followed along.

"See that hill?"

He took my arm, and extending his other hand, pointed across the water. A tree-covered hill rose above the woods in the distance. He stood very close to me, and something fluttered in my stomach. What was my heart doing down there?

I gulped and nodded.

"That's the Overlook," he said. "You get an amazing view of the lake from up there, but you can't drive up. You have to hike. In fact, there are trails all around the lake."

"It's peaceful here," I said. "It feels like a place where nothing bad could ever happen."

Anthony let go of my arm. "Something bad did happen once. The only other murder investigation I've worked was here." He looked off into the middle distance, thinking. "It looked like a drowning accident at first. But it turned out to be murder."

"Don't tell me," I said. "You found saltwater in his lungs."

Anthony's eyes widened. "How did you know?"

"Lucky guess."

It was a lucky guess. But then the writers of *Silver & Gold* must have gotten the plot idea from the news. Could it have been a small local story from Carmine they found online? Considering how the writers trawled the news for plot ideas for the many seasons of the show, it wasn't inconceivable. But it was a little creepy—like Eve Silver's on-screen story was alive and well in Carmine.

I only hope Adam Gold doesn't turn up, I thought to myself. *Or rather, his brother.*

As I gazed out over the water, I caught sight of a canoe. A single person sat in the craft, paddling steadily, switching from side to side.

Anthony shaded his eyes with one hand. "That looks like Liz Lewis."

"Lewis?" I asked. "Any relation to Mark Lewis?"

"Sure. Liz is—or was—his aunt."

We watched her canoe cut through the calm waters as she headed for shore. She didn't steer toward the dock where we stood, instead heading for a cluster of rocks to the left of the beach. As we watched her land, and then expertly jump out and heave the canoe up over the rocks, Anthony explained that Liz lived alone in the woods.

"She's a loner," he said. "She mostly avoids people."

"Were she and Mark friendly?"

"Was Mark friendly with anyone?" He shook his head. "I don't think they spent much time together, at least recently. If I remember correctly, Liz used to have something to do with Cafe Roma. But that was years ago. Hey, Bernie," he eyed me closely, "you know I'm happy to talk, but I can't share details about the investigation."

I avoided his gaze. "I know that."

"Good. And while we're on the topic, we've gone over Mark's possessions, and what was in the cafe. Someone mentioned a book he was reading..."

"*A Moron's Step-by-Step Guide to Living with Less.*"

"That sounds right. Any idea where it might be?"

"It's gone?"

He shrugged. "Mark may have finished it and gotten rid of it. Or it's in a place we've overlooked. Probably not important, anyway."

He led me back through the boathouse and down to the beach, waxing lyrical about summer days at the lake, and then, seeing the charred remains of a bonfire near the lifeguard tower, he complained about the irresponsibility of teenagers. He picked up a couple of empty beer cans.

"When you were a kid, were you a boy scout?"

His eyebrows shot up. "Hey, how did you know that?"

"Lucky guess."

As he cleaned up, I gazed into the woods. Soon, he asked if I was ready to head back to town. But the appearance of Liz Lewis had sparked my curiosity. At the end of the beach, a path cut into the woods, heading in the direction I had seen Liz pull her canoe.

"Is that one of the hiking trails?" I asked, pointing.

"Want to take a look?" he asked. He glanced at his watch. "I've still got time, if you do."

I hesitated. Angelica might wonder just how long a lunch I could take. Not a good impression on the first day of work. I ought to head back. But part of me needed to go into those woods.

I dug out my phone. I'd saved Angelica's phone number,

and that of the bakery. After a couple of rings, she answered. Before I was halfway through explaining, she said, "Bernie, take as long a break as you want. I'm glad you're getting to see Carmine—it's important to get to know your home."

Home. I tried not to dwell on how much promise that word held, since my time in Carmine might be brief.

I hung up.

Together, Anthony and I took the path into the woods. Light filtered through the leaves of the trees, dappling the ground. Roots cut across the trail. We had to step carefully to avoid twisting an ankle. The trail never strayed far from the lake, and I had a clear view of its waters on my right.

Peering into the trees on the left, I caught sight of something white. Or rather off-white.

"Is that a trailer?"

"That's Liz Lewis's home," Anthony said.

High-end trailer homes could be first-class living on wheels. But this was a small, inexpensive aluminum box lifted off the ground by stacks of frieze blocks. Rusted junk lay scattered around it, along with Liz's canoe and an old battered bicycle leaning against a tree. There wasn't anything first class about it; it looked more like the end to a very bumpy journey.

My curiosity tugged at me again. If Anthony hadn't been here, I would have crept closer, but I didn't want to seem too interested, in case it got back to Chief Tedesco.

So we continued along the trail for another 15 minutes, admiring the nature, until I admitted to Anthony that I was growing tired and wouldn't mind heading back.

"Yeah, me too. I've got a report to write."

"About me?"

To his credit, he winced. "Yeah."

I put a hand on his arm. "It's all right, Anthony. You're doing your job."

He gave me a small smile and a nod.

"This part of my job isn't so bad," he said.

His words tempted me to leave my hand where it was. But I withdrew, and we enjoyed an awkward silence. Maybe he'd felt the same temptation.

"It's a good thing to have a friend," he said. "Especially a cop friend."

A thrill swept through me, and it was only partly to do with our moment of intimacy. My wish—that even as I felt surrounded by enemies, Anthony could be a friend—appeared to have come true.

We followed the trail back toward the beach and the boathouse, and as we caught sight of Liz Lewis's trailer again, Anthony broke the silence. "Doesn't look very nice, does it? I don't know how she does it. Especially her. See, Liz didn't always live in a trailer. She used to live in one of the fanciest old Victorians on Cedar Hill. This was back when I was a little kid. But she and her business partner got in a fight over money, and Liz stabbed him. It was a big deal in town and people talked about it for years."

"What happened?" I asked. "Did she go to jail?"

He nodded. "She faced homicide, but they downgraded it to manslaughter when the evidence was clear she acted in self defense. Apparently her business partner had tried to stab her first. They sentenced Liz to up to 10 years in prison, but she only served a year."

I stopped. "And then she moved out here?"

"That's right. After she got out, she moved out to this trailer in the woods. I'm not sure what happened. Maybe she lost everything and fell on hard times. Or maybe she decided to sell everything."

I thought of my desire to hide away after the Jay Casanova trial and wondered about that. Would poverty alone have sent Liz Lewis out into the woods? And right after serving her sentence? I didn't think so.

We left the woods, crossed the beach, and returned to the parking lot, where the only car was Anthony's cruiser. We both got in and, for a moment, we sat without the engine on.

"This was nice," I said, hoping to recapture the intimacy from earlier.

"Really nice," he said. He looked at me.

I didn't know how to return that look.

I had an uncomfortable flashback to a teenage date and shifted in my seat. I suddenly couldn't remember where to put my hands. In my lap? On my knees? Across my chest? Somehow I did it all the time, without thinking, and now it seemed like the most unnatural thing in the world.

Finally, after the silence between us had built to an unbearable crescendo, Anthony broke it.

"Bernie, I want you to know that—"

The crackle of his radio interrupted whatever he was going to say.

The voice of Chief Tedesco came through the speaker and hit me like a punch to the gut.

"Ferrante, you still got eyes on that Bernie Smyth girl?"

With a guilty glance at me, Anthony picked up the radio and pressed the button and said, "Uh, sure I do, chief."

"Good. Because we can't let her out of our sights." The radio crackled. *"She's guilty and we'll prove it. Consider it your top priority, you hear?"*

6

On the ride back to town, Anthony and I didn't speak a word to each other. His embarrassment was obvious.

Any lingering doubts I had about Chief Tedesco's intentions were gone. She was going to pin the murder on me, and not because I was an ideal suspect—it was because I had put her heartthrob in prison.

My mind felt like a pinball machine, every idea careening around, bouncing off walls, sounding alarms, slamming into dark holes from which they refused to return.

You should call Roberta.

No, I couldn't give up Carmine and go to the farthest reaches of Alaska.

You should ask Anthony for help.

No, he had his orders—he couldn't defy them. His chief had drawn the battle lines, and it was clear which side he must stand on.

You should report Chief Tedesco for misconduct.

For what? I had no concrete proof yet, only the suggestion of misconduct, and if I blew the whistle on her, wouldn't she simply reciprocate and reveal to the world who Bernie Smyth really was?

In fact, why hadn't she done so already? What was holding her back?

You should—you should...

I didn't know what I should do, and who else to turn to. I was beginning to think the only person I could rely on was myself.

As Anthony pulled the car over to the curb by Moroni's, he cleared his throat. "Chief Tedesco is a good cop. She's the most honest and diligent chief of police I know and she must have a reason—"

"Right. So honest and diligent that she's trying to pin a murder on an innocent person."

I took a deep breath and controlled my anger. At least what he'd said might explain why she hadn't revealed my secret: Chief Tedesco didn't blow my cover, because, in her own mind, she was an upright cop who wouldn't breach her agreement with the U.S. Marshalls Service. Except her devotion to Jay Casanova had amplified her suspicion of me, making me the obvious suspect for Mark's murder.

"Bernie," Anthony said, reaching over and putting a hand on my shoulder. "I don't actually believe you did it."

I shrugged off his hand and slid out of the car seat. "That's wonderful, Anthony. Maybe you can convince your boss that's true."

I closed the door before he could say more, pushing it shut without much force, too exhausted to be mad at him. It was as if the Jay Casanova trial would never end. When would I be free of Jay's long shadow?

A great weight pressed down on me. My feet felt as

heavy as rocks as I shuffled through the front door of Moroni's.

As soon as I stepped inside, however, something strange happened. A wave of cookie-scented air washed over me, and the weight on my shoulders crumbled and fell away. I took a deep breath, savoring the smell.

I exhaled. It was like ridding my body of noxious fumes, replacing them with sweetness.

Angelica came toward me. She held out an apron that said, "Moroni's Italian Bakery." She shook it, loosening flour and powdered sugar, and it sent up a cloud of white dust. As the sweet mist drifted down, the light struck it just so, and for an instant, I swear it looked as if Angelica had a halo around her head.

"Welcome back," she said with a glowing smile.

In that moment, in spite of everything, I had the odd sense that I was safe. I was home. I grabbed the apron and tied it around my waist.

"Put me to work," I said.

~

Angelica was behind the counter, carefully arranging cookies in the display case. She placed little handwritten cards next to each tray that named the Italian delicacies. She filled a bowl with biscotti and set it on top of the counter near the cash register. The card she put next to it said, "Take one—it's free!"

"Moroni's is nothing like Cafe Roma," I told her.

"Poor Mark. He didn't know how to be happy and now he's dead and gone. Which reminds me. You should read his obituary in *The Carmine Enquirer*."

I got out my phone and found *The Carmine Enquirer* website. The top post on Peter's news blog was Mark's obit.

Mark Lewis, owner of Cafe Roma in Carmine, New Jersey, died on Tuesday morning. He was 43 years old.

Mark was a well-known local business owner, whose Cafe Roma on Garibaldi Avenue attracted locals and tourists alike as well as feisty competition. An anonymous source has revealed to The Carmine Enquirer *that Cafe Roma and Moroni's Italian Bakery had an ongoing feud, which involved a threat of legal action from Carmine's own Parisi & Parisi, Attorneys at Law.*

"What's this about a feud between you and Mark?" I asked Angelica.

"Peter likes to make everything sound so sensational."

"So it's not true."

"Oh, it's true. See, Mark was buying baked goods from Moroni's, photographing them, and then using them in his advertising. It seemed foolish to me. In the end, the customers would be disappointed. If anything, he made it painfully obvious what a big difference there was between his cannoli and the real thing at Moroni's. For me, the worst thing was how he took advantage of the customers, serving them terrible coffee and baked goods."

"So you decided—what?—to send a cease-and-desist letter?"

"It was Dan Russo from Russo's Realty—he and I sit on the Chamber of Commerce together with Joanna Parisi—who convinced me to take action. I agreed Joanna could send the letter, though I didn't think it would do much good."

"Why not?"

"Mark was a bully. If you threatened him, he only got more aggressive."

"Would he have fought you in court?" I asked.

"Who knows? In any case, I never would have sued him, and he probably knew that." She cocked her head and gave me a sad smile. "At the end of the day, Bernie, what matters is how sweet you make your life. Mark preferred everything to be sour. A court case would be another bitter thing he could relish. I wasn't willing to turn my sweet life into a sour mess just because he was provoking me."

I continued reading the obit.

Beyond his business, Mark had a passion for nature and was often seen kayaking on Carmine Lake. He will also be remembered for his charitable donations to Mamma Mia's, a non-profit supporting single mothers in need.

Mark is survived by an aunt, Liz Lewis, and a cousin, Susan Davis.

I looked up from the article.

"Did you know about Mark donating to charity?"

Angelica shook her head. "It's nice to think that deep down he really was a generous human being. You know, I believe everyone is. Maybe some pain makes them act in cruel ways, but underneath, aren't we all good?"

I must have gaped at her, because she asked me, "What? Do I have something in my hair?"

"No, no, nothing."

I'd never heard a person share a life philosophy that was so optimistic. If it had been anyone but Angelica, I would have suspected it was a hoax, but it was obvious she was serious.

It made me like her even more.

In his obit, Peter was no doubt hinting that Angelica might have a motive for murder. She was no more a murderer than I was. In fact, she didn't seem to have a murdering bone in her body. Just a lot of confectioner's sugar.

The bell over the front door jingled.

Nat appeared, a big grin on his face. He swept aside his bangs, which had, as usual, fallen over his glasses.

"Ladies."

"Good timing, Nat," Angelica said. "You can keep an eye on customers while I give Bernie another rundown of the bakery."

Angelica reminded me where everything was located. The drawer with menus—there was a large overhead board but also individual booklets patrons could flip through—plus, the cupboard with takeout bags and boxes. She showed me her little office to the right of the bakery. Then gave me another walkthrough of the many functions on the industrial-sized ovens.

"But don't worry if you can't remember it all—I'll always be here to get things started in the morning. I start my day at dawn so I can get my baking done," she explained, as we returned to the cafe at the front.

"You must have been here at the bakery when I got to Cafe Roma and found Mark's body."

Nat was leaning against the counter, drinking a cup of coffee. "She saw you."

"Wait a minute." I turned to Angelica. "Were you the witness who informed the police you'd seen me knocking on the front door of Cafe Roma?"

Angelica nodded. "That was me. I'd been at the bakery for hours when I saw you. In fact, I was at work before Mark got to the cafe. His lights were on above Cafe Roma when I arrived. When he left his apartment and went to work, I couldn't tell you. By then, I was out back, my hands deep in cookie dough."

"All by yourself?"

"Carlo stopped by to lend me a hand for a while. Maybe he saw something when he went back over to his restaurant."

Nat was dipping a biscotti in his coffee.

"These are free of charge, right?"

"For you, the coffee is, too," Angelica said and smiled. "The biscotti are a special treat to commemorate Mark. The few times he set foot in Moroni's, he bought a biscotti. I know he chose biscotti because they were inexpensive and he liked things that were cheap. But once he bit into the biscotti, he couldn't hide his enjoyment." She got a faraway, dreamy look in her eyes. "It's my belief that the moment anyone enjoys good Italian food, any meanness vanishes for an instant—the only thing that's left is the heavenly taste."

Whether or not that philosophy was true, offering free biscotti was a gracious gesture. Especially, as I told Angelica and Nat, because Mark did little to ingratiate himself with his neighbors.

"Mark made a lot of enemies over the years," Nat said, nodding.

"Anyone willing to kill him?" I asked.

"My goodness, no," Angelica cut in. "I don't think anyone in Carmine could do such a thing. The attack on Mark was obviously a burglary gone horribly wrong. It's the only explanation."

Nat raised an eyebrow at me, clearly as skeptical as I was. I knew a burglar wouldn't stop to drink an espresso with Mark before stabbing him in the back. Angelica clearly didn't like the idea of anyone in town being a killer.

"Speaking of enemies, Bernie," Nat said, chewing his biscotti. "I hear Chief Tedesco thinks you killed Mark Lewis."

"Nat Natale," Angelica berated him, clearly shocked. "That can't be true."

"Unfortunately, it's true," I said.

I explained how my panicked exit from the crime scene had made me look guilty, leaving out the bit about Chief Tedesco hating Bernadette Kovac for destroying Jay Casanova's reputation and putting him behind bars.

Angelica pressed a hand against her chest and gave me a worried look. "But Chief Tedesco will surely realize her mistake. Won't she?"

"She might need a little help," Nat said.

"What do you mean?" Angelica asked.

"Oh, you know, sometimes amateur detectives do a little snooping around, and they discover details the cops have overlooked. Like that TV show…"

"Which one?"

"You know, *Silver & Gold*."

I grabbed a cloth and rubbed the display counter glass, trying to look busy. I avoided meeting Nat's eyes.

"I like that show," Angelica said. "Too bad about that actor, Casanova, and his dealings with drugs and guns. Whatever happened to the actress?"

"Bernadette Kovac?" Nat shrugged. "Vanished after the trial. Like her character Eve Silver would have done. And I bet wherever she is now, she's still relying on her detective skills to solve mysteries. Maybe she could solve Mark Lewis's murder."

"You think so?" Angelica asked, clearly delighted.

A bolt of lightning struck me—or might as well have. I

nearly dropped the cloth. I looked up at Nat. He sipped his cup of coffee, seemingly oblivious to my stare.

He'd said, "I bet wherever she is now, she's still relying on her detective skills to solve mysteries."

The idea, I realized, had been germinating in my own mind, but I'd been unable to put words to it. I'd already been asking questions, trying to get information out of Anthony, snooping around Liz Lewis's trailer, paying close attention to what Angelica had to say about Mark Lewis.

It was a familiar way of thinking—Eve Silver's way of piecing together a puzzle. For years, I had inhabited her mind. Slipping back into the role would feel good.

"Maybe she could solve Mark Lewis's murder," Nat had said.

Well, why not? If no one did anything to find the actual killer, Chief Tedesco would pin the murder on me. Why shouldn't I take action?

The bell over door jingled and customers—a whole busload of tourists—came bustling in.

"Ready to get to work?" Angelica asked.

I grinned. "I've never been more ready in my life."

7

As soon as Angelica opened the door, the customers came streaming in. For a bakery in such a small town, Moroni's made a brisk business. Angelica explained that her reputation had spread to other towns in the county and even to New York City, and people didn't mind taking a drive an hour or more to pick up a box of cannoli.

"The cannolis are the most popular," she said with a smile. "They always sell out."

Soon, I saw it for myself. One tourist wanted pignoli, another rainbow cookies, a third pizzelle, but every one of them ordered cannolis.

Could they really be so good?

Angelica put one on a plate and handed it to me. "If you're going to work at Moroni's, you have to love my baked goods."

The cannoli consisted of a dough shell, deep fried until it was crisp, with little bubbles on the outside. The shell was then stuffed with a sweet ricotta filling and additions, such as pistachios or chocolate chips.

Mine had pistachio. I licked the end of the cream filling. It melted in my mouth—the ideal balance between sweet and savory, with the soft crunch of pistachios preparing me, as I took a big bite, for the perfect crackle of the shell.

"Oh, wow. What else can I say, but 'oh' and 'wow'?"

Angelica smiled. "Glad you like it."

I thought of Mark's cannoli. Now I understood why he'd put cannoli on his bare-bones menu, and then falsely advertised with photos of the ones from Moroni's. Angelica's cannoli had gained popularity, attracting out-of-towners, which Mark had then tried to lure into Cafe Roma. What a disappointment it must have been for Jane or John Doe, who'd come seeking a perfectly crisp shell with heavenly ricotta filling, when they tasted the soggy cannoli at Mark's cafe.

The bell over the door jingled and a woman I'd seen on the street stepped into the bakery, weaving her way through the gaggle of tourists.

"I need to find Liz Lewis," the woman said, speaking breathlessly as she fought her way to the counter. "But does she have a phone? No. Is she home when I go knocking on that trailer of hers? No." She let out a huff of frustration. "Has she come by the bakery to get bread? Well? Have you seen her, Angelica?"

Angelica smiled. "Calm down, Joanna. You know Liz spends half her days walking those woods or canoeing. She'll turn up."

I realized she must be Joanna Parisi from the law firm across the street. She had curly reddish brown hair, a wide mouth, and eyes ringed with heavy mascara.

"I saw her yesterday," I said.

"You did?" Joanna leaned on the counter, narrowing her eyes at me. "When and where did you see her? Was it here in town or in the woods? Did you talk? Did she say when she'd be back? Tell me everything."

"In the woods," I explained, somewhat overwhelmed by the barrage of breathless questions. "Yesterday afternoon, she came back to her trailer after canoeing. We didn't talk. She didn't even see me."

Joanna grimaced. "That trailer is a health hazard, an accident waiting to happen. Angelica, could I have an Americano, please?"

I told Angelica I would make it. As I stood by the espresso machine, filling the portafilter, Joanna kept talking.

"The thing is that as Mark Lewis's closest relative, she's set to inherit. Even though I told him a million times to get his house in order, the silly man didn't make a will, so now his assets—the cafe building, which he owned outright, his house, his car, his kayak, whatever else there is—it all gets doled out according to the intestate succession laws, and there's the 120-hour rule, you know. Well, you know."

"Joanna," Angelica said, not hiding her amusement. "I don't know."

Dark brown, almost black, liquid was pouring into the takeout cup. The rich, earthy smell wafted upward. Ah, the joy of making a proper Americano, not the watery stuff Mark had insisted I serve at Cafe Roma.

Meanwhile, I kept one ear open for what Joanna was saying.

"Well, here's how it works," she said. "The law defines a kind of hierarchy of kin, so you know who's next in line, and so long as you're still alive within 120 hours after the deceased dies, then you inherit everything. Then, if you die a week later, your kids or your other next of kin inherit. See?"

Angelica shrugged. She didn't quite see. But I thought I did.

"So if Liz is next in line," I said over my shoulder. "Then she'll inherit and the assets will be part of her estate. But if she's had an accident, then the full inheritance passes on to the next person in Mark's line of inheritors."

Joanna snapped her fingers. "This kid is sharp, Angelica. Hold on to her."

At 32, I was hardly a kid. And she couldn't be a day over 40. But I had a feeling Joanna was the kind of person who called a lot of people "kid."

"I left a note on Liz's door with my name and number, telling her to call me urgently," Joanna said. "*Urgently*. Do you think she knows that word?"

Clearly, Joanna knew the word. Maybe she applied it to most things in her life. Did she really need more caffeine? Well, she was a grownup and could decide for herself. I topped off the espresso shots with hot water and placed the cup on the counter.

Joanna put a lid on the cup and dropped a five-dollar bill on the counter.

"Keep the change."

She took a sip and closed her eyes. "And she knows how to make good coffee. I'm telling you, Angelica, she's a keeper."

Then she swept out of the bakery with a "have a good day" and she was gone.

"She's a whirlwind," Angelica said.

"A talking whirlwind."

"Above all, she's a happy customer. Well done, Bernie."

I failed to suppress a grin. It was impossible not to bask in Angelica's approval. And so I was grateful to Joanna on two fronts: She'd provided interesting information on Mark's will (however unprofessional her spilling those details might be) and she'd complimented my Americano, giving me a much-needed confidence boost.

Bernie the Barista was off to a good start. So was Eve Silver, private detective.

∽

Though no more tour groups came our way that afternoon, a steady stream of customers filed in and out of the front door. The poor bell got a serious workout, jingling every few minutes. In a couple of hours, I boxed up more cannolis than I'd ever seen in my life.

"If this keeps up, we'll run out," I said.

"Which is why I'll teach you how to make cannolis," Angelica said as she filled a bag with pignoli cookies.

"That sounds dangerous," I said. "I'm not sure I'll be able to resist eating each cannoli I make."

Angelica laughed. "We'll need to make so many for the cannoli competition at the street fair that there's no way you'll have time to eat your way through the batch."

She'd told me about the annual Carmine Italian Street Festival. Usually occurring on Labor Day weekend, it marked the official end of summer, the beginning of fall, and it brought visitors from all across the state. The town had become famous for its Italian delicacies and the fair included competitions for the best fresh pasta and, yes, cannolis. Moroni's would compete against bakeries from other towns, even other counties.

"Are you nervous?" I asked Angelica.

"Sure am," she said. "If I weren't, it would mean I didn't have my heart in it."

One of my acting coaches had told me exactly that when I was starting out in film and TV, and it put a smile on my face. It seemed bakers and actors had more in common than I'd imagined.

The bell over the door jingled again, and a man walked in. He wore a brown plaid sport coat over a yellow shirt. The yellow did his face no favors. It was round, suggesting he enjoyed his food and drink, and had a greasy sheen to it. So did his hair, which had been slicked back with what must have been a whole tub of pomade.

Angelica introduced him as Dan Russo.

"From Russo's Realty," Dan said and shook my hand.

I had seen his offices down the street. In fact, on our tour of the town, Anthony Ferrante had pointed it out and mentioned that Dan was Carmine's only realtor and a significant contributor to the town's business. He was also the head of the local Chamber of Commerce.

Dan ordered a coffee, and I got started on making an Americano.

"How's business?" Angelica asked him.

"Well, Mark's death won't do us any favors, especially right before the street fair. Bad timing."

That struck me as insensitive. Angelica reacted too.

"Dan, we're talking about a man dying."

"I know, I know," Dan said, holding up his hands to show he meant no harm. "It's a tragic business, but you gotta see my side of things. The town's reputation isn't the only thing at stake. There's also the sale of the cafe."

"Oh? I didn't know the cafe was for sale."

That jolted me. I remembered Peter's comment: "Rumor has it that Mark wants to sell the cafe." Maybe it explained his tight-fisted, short-sighted way of running things—had he not cared about unhappy customers walking away because his plan was to sell the cafe?

"Nobody knew the cafe was for sale," Dan said. "Mark wanted to keep it quiet. But we had a buyer, and we were going to move forward. Within a few weeks, the deal would have been done. Mark would have moved out in a few months."

What had Mark told me when he urged me to save on coffee beans? "Cut that in half and I can make my current inventory last another three months." He'd snapped at me when I'd asked what was happening in three months, probably because I'd come close to learning his secret. In three months, he'd expected to have sold the cafe.

"I have no idea what will happen now," Dan complained. "I guess it depends on who inherits."

"I heard Liz Lewis is the next of kin."

"Yes, Joanna told me that too."

As I filled a cup with two espresso shots, I thought, *Wow, people do gossip a lot in this town*. It seemed Joanna had told everyone that Liz would inherit. Was that even legal, sharing all that information? I didn't mind. For my own purposes, it was helpful. If the new Eve Silver simply had to stand behind a counter and wait for gossip to reach her, this amateur sleuthing wouldn't turn out to be so difficult.

"Guess I'll have to talk to Liz," Dan said, rubbing his chin and looking unsure.

"I can't imagine she would want to hold on to the cafe, Dan."

"But that doesn't mean she'll want to go through with the deal I've been negotiating."

"Why not?"

Dan hesitated. "Well, I can't really tell you. It wasn't just

Mark who wanted to keep this under wraps. The buyer is secretive too."

This was getting more and more interesting. I topped the espresso shots with hot water and turned to the counter, sliding the cup toward Dan.

"Is the cafe worth a lot of money?" I asked, trying to sound only casually interested.

"Property values have shot up, and Garibaldi Avenue only has a few storefronts," Dan said. "So yes, it stands to sell for a fair amount."

If the cafe was worth a lot of money, would someone kill for it? Or would someone kill to keep Mark from selling?

Before I could ask more questions, Angelica leaned across the counter and grabbed the cup of coffee.

"Oh, dear," she said. "Bernie, this is too much."

Confused, I watched her remove the cup from Dan's reach, and I had a brief flashback to Mark Lewis scolding me about using too much coffee in the Americano.

"But an Americano needs two shots," I said, trying not to sound defiant, and probably failing.

"Of course it does, sweetie. But Dan likes a *caffe lungo*, not an Americano."

"A caffe lungo?" I asked. I felt like a kid on the first day of school, clueless and embarrassed.

"It's a single espresso shot run through the machine with more water. Basically, a long espresso or a small coffee. Here, I'll show you."

Angelica got out a small coffee cup, slightly larger than an espresso cup. She added grounds to the portafilter, tamping down enough coffee for a single shot of espresso, then ran the machine. But instead of stopping after 1 ounce of espresso, she continued to run the machine, pouring another whole ounce of water through the grounds until the little cup filled.

"See, this is a caffe lungo. The perfect coffee for the busy person who wants more than an espresso."

"The perfect coffee for me," Dan said. "Espresso's leave me thirsting for more, and an Americano takes too long to drink."

Angelica put a comforting hand on my arm. "Don't worry. Soon you'll learn what everyone in town likes to drink and nibble on, and there's an entire menu of coffees to choose from."

She gestured at the menu board above us. I'd assumed that the many additional coffee names were dessert coffees, specialized stuff we'd rarely need to use. But I could see I still had a lot to learn: espresso, lungo, ristretto, macchiato, corretto, cappuccino, latte, and more.

"I'll study the menu and promise that—"

"Bernie," Angelica said, cutting me off. "There's no need to study or make promises. You've got time to learn. You're not rushing off, are you?"

I'd be rushing off to prison if Chief Tedesco got her way, but I didn't tell Angelica that. I shook my head.

"Good. Then take this tray of cannoli, please, and deliver them to my brother Carlo next door. He'll need them for the dinner crowd later today. Dan and I will take a few minutes to talk about Chamber of Commerce stuff."

Behind us stood a tall bakery rack on wheels. Rows of cannolis lined one of the metal trays. I slid the tray out, and maneuvering around the counter, carried it toward the door. Despite Angelica's encouragement, I couldn't help but feel I was being dismissed after a poor performance. It made me realize how much I wanted to show Angelica my appreciation for the job.

As I pulled open the front door and the bell jingled softly, I overheard Dan say, "I'm beginning to feel this year's street fair is a make it or break it moment for our town..."

It left me with another thing to worry about. But also an opportunity: If the street fair was so important, maybe helping Angelica prepare would be my chance to shine.

8

As soon as I entered Carlo's Restaurant, my worries about making the right kind of coffee vanished. The carpeted floors softened my step. The heavy velvet drapes framing the front windows muted the sounds within. Low music played from hidden speakers: a breathy brush of drums, a trickle of piano notes, a trumpet twittering softly. A couple stragglers from lunch lingered over their coffee, a man and a woman leaning across the white tablecloth, speaking in hushed tones.

But the gentle bubble broke when a loud voice cut through the quiet.

"You can't be serious, Maria."

A short, bald man with a black goatee stood by the bar at the back. He threw up his hands in exasperation.

The woman next to him was Maria Ferrante. She'd crossed her arms on her chest and was giving the man a raised eyebrow that suggested profound skepticism. I recalled seeing her argue with Mark in the street.

"I'm dead serious, Carlo," she said.

"What other secrets have you been hiding from me?"

The man called Carlo—that must be Angelica's brother—turned and saw me approaching with the tray full of cannolis.

"Ah, the cannolis have arrived," he said. "And so has an independent judge."

He whisked the tray out of my hands and set it on the counter next to two small Pyrex baking dishes. Both appeared to contain lasagna.

"This," Carlo said, pointing out the dish on the left, "is my famous Italian lasagna. Ground beef. Tomato sauce. Topped off with béchamel sauce. As it's done in Italy."

He gave Maria a pointed look.

"This," Maria said, pointing out the dish on the right, "is my family's recipe for Italian-American lasagna. Ground beef. Tomato sauce. Ricotta and mozzarella. Any fool knows this is the real deal."

"Ha!" Carlo scoffed. "Let our independent judge decide for herself. Which should we serve as tonight's dinner special?"

He handed me a fork.

"Eat and speak the truth."

Unable—and frankly unwilling—to resist the invitation, I scooped up a bite of the Italian lasagna with béchamel sauce.

The baked béchamel had caramelized on top, the sweetness immediately cut by a tangy tomato sauce and the richness of the meat. The balance was perfect. Unable to restrain myself, I groaned with pleasure.

Carlo beamed. "See? I told you so, Maria."

"Slow your roll, Carlo. She hasn't tasted mine yet."

Maria handed me a glass of water and Carlo explained, "A bit of water to clear your palate."

After a sip of water, I dug into Maria's Italian-American lasagna and brought the fork to my mouth.

There was no sweetness in this one. It was layer upon layer of rich savory, from the mozzarella and ricotta down through the tomato and beef. When I'd finished chewing, I let out a long sigh of satisfaction, and Maria patted me on the back.

Smiling, she said, "See, Carlo? Told you so. My lasagna makes people yearn for more."

"But which is superior?" Carlo asked.

They both looked at me.

I closed my eyes, recalling both the béchamel and the mozzarella-ricotta versions.

"Honestly? They both win."

"Bah!" Carlo threw up his hands and laughed. "You are a lousy judge, but an excellent neighbor. So it's up to me to decide—and I don't want to."

"So what do we do?" Maria asked.

Carlo looked thoughtful. Then his eyebrows rose, and he held up a finger, having apparently come up with a solution.

"We serve both. Give people the choice of an Italian or an Italian-American lasagna. You can never have too much lasagna."

"I'll make more of both, boss."

Maria smiled and picked up the Pyrexes and carried them past the bar and through a swinging door to the kitchen beyond.

Carlo leaned close to me and, shielding his mouth with one hand, as if to keep his whisper a secret, said, "Maria has a forceful personality. If I didn't humor her, I'd have hell to pay. Besides, I love giving my customers choices."

He thanked me for bringing the cannolis and added, "Of

course I already know who you are. Angelica has told me everything. *Poverina*, it must have been such a shock for you to find Mark."

He kept his voice low, occasionally glancing toward his customers, no doubt worried that the mention of murder would frighten them. I told him it had been an enormous shock.

"I don't understand who would want to kill Mark," I said, fishing for his opinion.

"My sister believes it could have been a burglary," Carlo said. "But I've heard no one say they saw strangers in the area that morning, and if what I hear is true, the attack happened during the morning hours. Not the best time for a burglary."

I agreed with him, of course, but said nothing. The burglary theory made no sense.

"Unfortunately, Bernie, I saw nothing. But then I spent the early morning in the back of my sister's bakery. I was helping her make cannolis and cookies. Then I came here and began making sauce."

That corroborated Angelica's story. Unless they were in cahoots and providing an alibi for each other, I could rule them out. Did Carlo even have a reason to kill Mark?

"Did you know Mark well?" I asked.

"Not really. He rarely came to my restaurant to eat, because he found the menu too—how do I put this?—expensive. He only came when someone else paid. In fact, the last time I saw him, he was having lunch with someone who picked up the check."

"Who was it?"

Carlo shrugged. "I don't know. An out-of-towner that I didn't recognize. They sat at a corner table, and at first I paid little attention to them. But after a while, I noticed raised voices, and suddenly Mark shot to his feet, threw down his napkin, and pointed a finger at the man. 'The cafe will never be yours', he shouted, and then stormed out. A moment later, the man paid and left."

"Did he come back?"

Carlo shook his head. "I haven't seen him since."

∼

Walking down the sidewalk to Moroni's, I considered what I'd learned.

Before his death, Mark had planned to sell the cafe. He had met a mystery man at Carlo's and vowed the man would never get the cafe. Get it how, though? Had the man offered to buy it? According to Dan, Mark had found a buyer, and they were about to move forward with the deal when the murder happened. What if Mark had threatened to pull out? Would the mystery buyer have killed for that? Or some other potential buyer? Hardly. Killing Mark wouldn't help them get their hands on the cafe.

As soon as I opened the door to Moroni's, my speculation had to be put on hold. A long line of customers crowded the doorway, and I had to push my way past them and rush behind the counter to come to Angelica's aid.

"Oh, thank goodness you're back," she said.

The late-afternoon rush was upon us. Some customers wanted to sit and drink coffee and nibble on a cookie or a cannoli. Even more people bought treats to go.

One couple in their seventies—both with stark white hair and smiles that deepened their wrinkles—explained that they'd driven a full hour and a half from Essex County to bring home some of Moroni's famous cannoli.

As she boxed up half a dozen cannoli, Angelica told them about the upcoming street festival.

"We'll be there," the husband said.

"And we'll tell our friends and family," the wife said.

Word of mouth was spreading about Moroni's. I could see why Angelica had been struggling to run the bakery on her own. As soon as one crowd had been served, more people came jostling through the door.

Angelica pushed a loose strand of hair behind one ear and let out a huff. "Phew, looks like it's finally calming down."

The display case had big empty spots, trays littered with crumbs rather than heaps of cookies. We were running dangerously low on napkins and takeout boxes. My back and arms ached from standing and stretching and bending down to get things from the low cupboards.

As I put a hand to my lower back and winced, Angelica made a sympathetic sound. "It's hard work, but you'll sleep like a baby tonight."

When the steady influx of customers finally slowed to a trickle, and then the bakery emptied, Angelica flipped the sign to say, "Sorry, We're Closed."

Then she shepherded me out back to the kitchen.

"Let's make some cannolis," she said. "The street fair is on Saturday. That's in three days. If we're going to be ready, we both need to be cannoli-making machines. We'll try out a few now, and then tomorrow morning you can help me make a whole batch. What do you say?"

I rolled up my sleeves. "Let's do it."

Angelica showed me how to make cannolis, step by step. First, we had to make the long and round shells, which we would fill with the ricotta cream.

"It's simple," she said. "Flour, sugar, a little salt, cocoa powder, butter. Then it sits in the fridge for a few hours."

Angelica opened the fridge in the kitchen and got out a bowl with dough she'd already prepared.

We rolled the dough and shaped it into little disks, which we then wrapped around metal cannoli tubes.

"Next, we heat the oil in this pot and lower the tubes in."

I watched as Angelica demonstrated. She showed me how to turn the tubes. The dough was already turning brown and crisp, with little bubbles forming on the outside.

"See the bubbles? That's a sign we're doing it right."

After the dough turned a deep brown, we used tongs to fish them out of the pot and lay them on paper towels to soak up the excess oil.

"While they cool, let's make the ricotta filling." Angelica brought out a big tub of ricotta and measured up sugar in a bowl. "I've strained this ricotta ahead of time to make it nice and thick. Now we mix the sugar in."

While I stirred the ricotta and sugar in the bowl, Angelica lined up three small vintage green Pyrex mixing bowls. One contained chocolate chips, the second chopped pistachio nuts, the third candied fruit.

"Some people like to mix the chocolate chips or nuts or fruit into the filling, but I believe less is more. I prefer to let the ricotta work its magic."

She filled a piping bag with the ricotta mixture and then squeezed the cream into one of the shells. Lifting the shell, she dipped one end into the pistachios and then the other end too.

"Just so."

The cannoli was done. The crisp shell contained the rich ricotta filling decorated with chopped pistachios at either end.

"It's so simple," I said, surprised. "What makes yours so different from others?"

"What makes mine worth driving for? It's the small touches. The quality of ricotta. The flour, and how I strain it. The amount of sugar and the kind of butter. Good baking is about hard work, Bernie. Great baking is hard work combined with delicious, high-quality ingredients." She paused and a smile spread across her face. "Well, that and a dash of love."

The phone rang out front, and Angelica left me to work on the cannolis. I piped the ricotta filling into another shell and dipped the ends in chocolate chips. Even I could figure this out.

When Angelica came back to the kitchen to check on me, she rubbed her hands together.

"Ooh," she cooed. "That looks ready to eat."

I bit my lip. This was the master of cannoli speaking. She would be disappointed. I knew it. Somehow, even with a simple task like this, I must have screwed it up.

She picked up the cannoli, turned it this way and that, studying its form, nodding approvingly. She took a big bite. I'd expected her to take a small, dainty bite. Not Angelica. She opened wide and chomped down, like a shark, and chewed with obvious relish.

"This is good, Bernie," she said. "We did good. Crunchy shell. Rich filling—not too dense and not too sweet—and the ratio of cream to chocolate chip is perfect. I think you may have the magic touch."

I'd done almost nothing, yet basked in the compliment. It was like having a favorite teacher in school give me an A on a paper. I felt like doing a little happy dance.

"Now you just need to make three hundred of these," she said, sprinkling powdered sugar on the cannoli.

That stopped my mental happy dance.

"Three hundred?"

"The street festival will bring hundreds of tourists to town, and we'll need enough for the bakery, a stand at the fair, and Carlo's Restaurant."

Thinking of Carlo's brought back thoughts of what Angelica's brother had said about Mark and the mystery man. I shared my thoughts with Angelica.

"People had made offers on the cafe before," she said. "Dan told me that long ago. It's not surprising. I get offers too, especially as Carmine's property values have increased. Cafe Roma's in a prime location with lots of potential, but Mark turned them all down. Whoever got him to change his mind must have been persuasive."

That was what I had been thinking. Unless something else persuaded him. A threat, maybe? But that seemed unlikely. Mark was a bully and would respond to a threat with aggression. Who was the mystery buyer Dan wouldn't talk about—and was it the same stranger who'd treated Mark to lunch at Carlo's?

"Do you have any idea who the man Mark met with could have been?" I asked Angelica.

Angelica shook her head. "No idea. And if Carlo didn't recognize him, he's not only from out of town, he's someone who hasn't visited much."

I let out a sigh. Angelica was right. But if he rarely came to town, how would I discover who the mystery man was?

9

At the Old Mill, I looked around. Half a dozen people stood in the bar, others sat in the booths. Nat had invited me for an "after hours" drink, but he hadn't arrived yet, so I settled onto a barstool.

I caught half my reflection in the mirror behind the rows of liquor bottles. I had confectioner's sugar in my hair and streaks of chocolate on my cheeks. Every muscle in my body ached. Since I didn't own a car, I'd walked all the way to the Old Mill, and that hadn't made me any less sore. I ought to have gone home, stood under a hot jet of water in the shower for half an hour, and then put myself to bed.

But I wanted the company. Someone to talk to. My mind was such a swirl of clues and theories. I needed to learn more about this mystery or I wouldn't be able to sleep a wink. Plus, my belly rumbled, demanding a refuel after all the hard work.

Jerry, the bartender, gave me one of his silent greetings and a raised eyebrow, his way of asking what I wanted.

"Food first," I said. "And a tall glass of ice water, please."

Since the Old Mill didn't serve food, I'd brought along a

takeout burrito with chips and salsa. I unfolded the butcher's paper and grabbed the burrito. I took a huge bite and washed it down with ice water.

While I ate at the bar, I watched the TV screen above the rows of liquor bottles. The news came on. There was no sound, which was fine by me. I preferred to listen to the music—Springsteen was singing about Rosie being the one—and read the captions instead.

After headlines about politics came trial footage showing Jay Casanova in handcuffs as they escorted him out of the courtroom.

The screen cut to Harry Casanova, Jay's brother and business partner. The caption below the image said, "Harry Casanova wanted for questioning."

Another image appeared, and it made me tense. The photo was of me.

"Well, if it isn't Eve Silver," a voice said behind me.

I coughed, food stuck in my throat, and dropped my burrito on the open butcher's paper on the bar.

Nat came to my side and slapped my back.

"Whoa there," he said. "Didn't mean to startle you, Bernie."

I took a big gulp from my drink, my eyes watering.

He sat down on the stool next to mine and cocked his head, studying me. "You all right?"

For a moment I thought you'd recognized me as Eve Silver and it nearly gave me a heart attack. No, I'm not all right.

I didn't say that, of course.

"You surprised me."

"What can I say? I'm full of surprises." He stared up at the TV screen. "First Bernadette Kovac disappears, then Harry Casanova. You think there's a connection?"

"I don't know..."

I could hardly speak the words. My mouth had gone dry. I took another gulp of water.

A montage was playing on the screen—clips culled from seven seasons of *Silver & Gold*. Eve Silver featured heavily, and there was one close-up of my face after another.

"That Eve Silver," Nat said admiringly.

There I was with blonde Marilyn Monroe-like hair and skin-tight outfits. I tried to make myself small at the bar, hoping no one else was watching the TV.

"Can I tell you a secret?" Nat said, leaning close to me. "I used to obsess over Adam Gold. Even now, I wonder, wouldn't it be cool to be a private detective? Wouldn't it be amazing to be like Adam Gold or Eve Silver?"

I nodded silently. Yes, it would. If only the world didn't realize I actually was Eve Silver.

The news shifted its focus to sports, and Nat turned his attention back to me.

"How's work?"

He pointed out the sugar in my hair, and we had a good laugh about occupational hazards. I relaxed again. When I asked him about his job at the historical society, he became animated and talked about the origins of Carmine—how an Italian immigrant had founded the township in the 1880s, its expansion with the sawmill and textile factories, and then post-World War II economic collapse, only to bounce back in the early 2000s as a kind of mecca for Italian-American culture.

"Carmine's come full circle," he said. "It started as a home for Italians in America, and in a way it has returned to its roots."

Nat and I were deep in conversation, and before I realized it, more and more people had arrived. The bar got crowded. The music competed with conversations, getting louder and louder.

I took a restroom break and passed the booths along the back wall, only to see Anthony sitting across from someone whose back was toward me. He was in his uniform. I called out his name, and he looked up, uncomfortable, and gave a little stiff wave. As I came alongside the booth, I realized why. He was sitting across from Chief Tedesco. She narrowed her eyes at me.

"Miss Smyth," she said, her voice as sharp as an ice pick. With those two words, she seemed to say, "I'm watching you. I know you did it. I'm going to get you."

I gave her a brief nod and then hurried to the restrooms.

When I returned to the bar, I promised myself to have one drink and then go home. The last thing I needed now was to attract any more negative attention—and that was the only attention I was getting from Chief Tedesco.

"Hey, did you see that Chief Tedesco is here?" Nat asked, as if he guessed what was on my mind.

I nodded. He leaned close to me.

"She asked me a bunch of questions about you. I don't know what you did, Bernie, but our chief of police has the hots for you—and I don't mean romantically."

"I know."

He patted my arm. "Don't worry. She may seem tough, but she's a softy on the inside. Only the other day, I saw her jogging down the street and she was wearing this ugly, pink t-shirt with a big heart on it. And guess whose face was inside the heart?"

It wasn't hard to guess, but I played Nat's game and shrugged.

"Jay Casanova." He grinned. "She's a huge fan. Now, if

that doesn't take the edge of her toughness, I don't know what does."

I nodded, my teeth gritted. I desperately wanted to change the topic and was glad when Nat pointed out that Maria had arrived. She stood at the far end of the bar talking to Emma, and I waved to them. Maria waved back, but Emma frowned and turned away. I wondered what I had done to offend her. I didn't even know her.

Seeing Maria brought back memories of my conversation with Carlo. And that set my thoughts swirling again: Who could have killed Mark?

"Maybe a burglar," Nat said when I asked him what he thought.

"In the half hour between my call and me finding Mark dead?" I shook my head. "A burglar would have seen that Mark had arrived and wouldn't risk going in. If you're going to break into a cafe, why not do it at night?"

"You've got a point," Nat said.

"Neither Angelica nor Carlo saw anything unusual that morning," I said. "Did you?"

He laughed. "Are you asking me if I have an alibi?"

My face grew hot. I hoped the bar was too dim to reveal my blush.

"It's all right, detective," Nat said with a wink. "I have nothing to hide. I was at my uncle's place having breakfast with him. Besides, I wasn't upset when Mark fired me, so why would I want to kill him?"

"I know," I said. "By the way, did you know Mark planned to sell?"

"Sell what? Better cannolis?"

I told him what I'd learned about the sale of the cafe and the mystery man at Carlo's. It felt good to share information with a friend. It felt good to have drinks and listen to music and talk. I'd missed companionship during the long months of the trial and then witness protection.

Nat frowned as he thought. "I have no idea who the mystery man could be. I guess someone could have killed Mark to get their hands on the cafe. But I agree, a buyer wouldn't do that. There's another obvious suspect, though, since she's set to inherit."

"Liz Lewis," I said, and he nodded. "Could anyone have seen anything that morning?"

He looked thoughtful. "Well, Joanna at Parisi & Parisi sometimes shows up early. Gino is at a conference this week, so he wasn't even around. Susan's almost always late. The law firm opens at 9:00 am sharp."

That left a sizable gap between the murder and the time when most people showed up. Nat detailed the other nearby businesses. Dan Russo opened his realtor's office at 9 am. Carlo rarely got going before 9 am, either. But he'd been getting to Moroni's early to help Angelica. Emma used to be up early at the bakery, but she stopped working the week before.

"I don't know who else would be around that early. Maybe cops on patrol. Mail delivery," Nat said. His face brightened. "Wait, I forgot someone. Maria. She doesn't start work until later, but she goes running in the mornings. Her route takes her down Garibaldi Avenue."

"When's that?"

"Usually between 6 and 7 am."

I had spoken with Mark at 6:11 am and found him around 6:30 am. If Maria had been jogging through town in the morning, she might have seen something.

Or even slipped into the cafe, killed Mark, and continued on her run.

Why had they fought in the street? The way Mark had

chased her suggested a lover's quarrel. If they'd been intimate, Mark might have made her an espresso as a gesture of kindness, maybe even a peace offering. But would she have a set of keys to the cafe? Mark's keys were on the counter and the back door was locked when I got to the cafe, suggesting the killer locked it from the outside.

When Nat went to the restroom, I sidled over to Maria and Emma and said hello.

Emma treated me to a sour grimace.

"I'll get us another round of drinks, Maria," she said, turning her back to me.

I didn't understand why Emma kept giving me the stink eye. Could she be mad at me for taking over at Moroni's? But that made no sense. She was leaving town for her graduate program, anyway.

I shook the thoughts off. My focus had to be on Maria right now.

"You know," Maria said, tilting her head and narrowing her eyes at me. "I get this strange feeling every time I see you, like we met long ago. Did you come to Carmine during the summers or something?"

Self-conscious, I touched my hair. My black hair. If she'd seen me with blonde hair, she'd instantly know why I looked familiar, especially with the TV playing footage from *Silver & Gold*.

I put on my best stage laugh. It sounded hollow. "Must be déjà vu. I've never been to this part of the state before." To change the topic, I quickly added, "But it sure is beautiful. I was out walking the other morning, admiring the trees and flowers. I may actually have seen you. Do you run in the mornings?"

Maria nodded. "Every morning around 6 am. On the weekends I run through the woods, but on weekdays I stick to town. Garibaldi is so peaceful before traffic gets going."

"We must have almost passed each other yesterday morning when I was heading to work. Before—"

"Before you found Mark?" She grimaced. "Yeah, I heard. Actually, you can't have seen me. I passed down Garibaldi later than usual, because I was walking, not running. See?"

She pulled up the leg of her jeans to reveal an ankle brace.

"I twisted my ankle. So I've been walking in the mornings to give it some rest. Doctor's orders."

"Maybe I was already inside the cafe."

She shrugged. "The shutters were partway up, but I didn't see anyone there. Just someone on a yellow bike down the street, but it turned off and headed up Cedar Hill. I was hobbling home before the police arrived." She shook her head slowly, sadly. "I can't believe what happened to Mark."

"It must have been a shock," I said sympathetically. I took a chance: "You two were close, weren't you?"

She nodded. "We were until we weren't."

"You had a falling out."

She laughed, a low, bitter laughter. "More like Mark pushed me off the cliff. When I first noticed him, I knew what people said about him—that he was mean and vindictive. A tough cookie. But to me, his gruffness seemed edgy, interesting. Well, that was before I started dating him. Oh, boy, did I learn my lesson. There was absolutely nothing romantic about his gruffness. He was a grouch. No more, no less. And all he could talk about was that damn cafe. Not like he loved the business. He complained about it, like it was a burden. I never understood why he held onto it, if it drove him so crazy."

Whatever had changed Mark's opinion, I thought, he

had decided to get rid of that burden, and it might have resulted in his death.

I studied Maria as she spoke, wondering if she could be the killer. She had a potential motive. But the killer, hearing me try the front door, must have bolted out the back. With her twisted ankle, Maria wouldn't have got away fast enough.

Some detail still eluded me. By staking out Garibaldi Avenue early in the morning, I might get an idea or two. Work at Moroni's started early anyway—no harm in snooping around before clocking in.

Emma returned with cocktails for her and Maria, but she kept her distance. She stood a few feet away, waiting, a sour frown on her face. The implication was clear. She didn't want to hang out with me.

Taking the hint, I said bye-bye and headed back to my spot at the bar, where Nat waited for me.

For a while, I stared at my drink.

Nat laughed. "Has the drink revealed its secrets yet?"

"I can't make sense of the locked door," I admitted. "There were two sets of keys, Mark's and mine, and both are accounted for. The killer must have locked the back door. But how did he get the keys?"

Nat laughed. "Oh, is that the big mystery?"

"What's so funny?"

He pulled out a keychain from his pocket and jingled it. "I still have my copies."

I gaped at him. "You mean Mark never asked for them back?"

Nat shrugged. "He was so busy kicking me out, maybe he forgot. The guy was sloppy."

Which meant Mark might have forgotten to reclaim other copies. Anyone could have had keys to the cafe.

10

The next morning, I'd hoped to beat Angelica to being the first in town. But standing outside Moroni's, I could see the curtains were parted. I didn't see her inside, though my gut told me she was already hard at work in the bakery out back. So did my nose: Wafts of baking cookies drifted out into the street.

Poor Angelica. The bakery was open 7 days a week. She worked and worked and worked—did she ever take a day off? Guilt tugged at my heart. I ought to be inside the bakery helping her on this Thursday morning, but I couldn't: I had to solve this mystery and clear my name or I'd be baking cookies at the Wessex County Correctional Facility.

A lone car floated down Garibaldi Avenue, and I ducked into the narrow alley between Moroni's Italian Bakery and Carlo's Restaurant. I waited for it to pass.

From my hiding place, I peered out across the street at Cafe Roma. Nothing happening at the corner of Poplar and Garibaldi. The crime scene tape was still in place and the cafe looked forlorn. I shuddered, remembering the body on the floor, the flames dancing from Mark's back.

Before I left home, I'd put on a baseball cap and a pair of sunglasses. In my experience, this was how you kept a low profile. In an episode of *Silver & Gold*, Eve Silver had worn a baseball cap and a pair of sunglasses when she trailed a suspect. Though, of course, that had been in the streets of San Francisco, not in small-town New Jersey.

I waited and watched. I yawned and wished I'd had the foresight to bring a cup of coffee. This stakeout stuff wasn't as easy as on TV.

Finally, at 6:32 am, a person appeared in the distance. The slight limp told me who it was before I could clearly see her face. It was Maria. She walked at a steady, brisk pace, yet as she came closer, I could tell she was being careful not to put too much pressure on her bad foot. No doubt her doctor wouldn't be impressed if he knew she still power walked every morning.

I hung back, waited, and watched as she passed on the opposite sidewalk.

Watching her, it occurred to me how easily someone could slip through the back of Cafe Roma without being seen. And slip out again. The killer, hearing me come, could have run fifty yards down Poplar and turned onto a side street, vanishing from view. Or simply hid behind the garbage cans.

My legs felt rubbery, my knees wobbly with sudden fear. I steadied myself against the wall. I might have walked right past the killer. He might have watched me from behind the garbage cans, then bolted before the cops arrived. He might have...

Enough. I cut off my thoughts. Did Eve Silver's knees get wobbly? Did she waste time worrying about dangers in the past? Not when there was a mystery to solve in the present.

I took a deep breath and straightened up.

I stuck my head further out to survey the street. Was anyone else in sight?

Just then a car swept past, windows down, music playing. Drums clashing, bass dropping bombs, and guitars noodling. The car—an old Honda Accord—slowed, and I saw Nat at the wheel. He waved at me and shouted, "Morning, Bernie!" Then he rolled on down Garibaldi toward the public library and the historical society.

I sighed. Guess I wasn't so inconspicuous after all.

A crash behind me made me jump. I spun around. The sound had come from an alleyway cutting across the one I was standing in.

I crept down the alley and stopped at the end, waiting a moment before daring to crane my neck and peer around the corner.

The alleyway cut behind Russo's Realty, Carlo's, and Moroni's—in fact, it ran parallel with Garibaldi Avenue behind all the businesses. It was the same kind of alley as the one behind Cafe Roma and offered space for garbage cans.

An old rusty bicycle lay on the ground, one wheel spinning. This must have been what had fallen and made the noise. Further down the alleyway, I caught sight of a person, and my heart thumped.

Grizzled hair. Patched jeans and a worn hunter's vest over a threadbare flannel shirt.

It was Liz Lewis.

She stood on the back steps of Moroni's with a duffel bag open, and Angelica was stuffing something into it. I looked closer, my heart beating fast. Oh no, was Angelica involved in something shady? What kind of trade were they making?

I couldn't help but think of Jay Casanova and the illicit

trade I had uncovered. Drugs. Guns. Was I about to stumble on another trafficking operation?

I blinked. Those weren't packets of cocaine or heroin. Or illegal guns. They were loaves of bread and rolls and paper bags, no doubt filled with cookies. Angelica finished handing the goods to Liz and Liz zipped up the bag.

From where I stood, I could hear Liz mumble a gruff "thank you." It didn't sound especially heartfelt, but Angelica gave Liz her usual warm smile and said, "Any time, Liz."

But Liz had already spun around. She swung the duffel back over her back, putting her arms through the straps so it hung like a rucksack on her back. She clomped back to the bicycle and heaved it off the ground.

I stepped back, trying to hide behind the corner, but a moment later, Liz was rolling out of the back alley on her bicycle.

She turned and saw me. "Mind your own damn business."

She swerved right past me, her rusty bicycle chain grinding, the wheels squeaking, as she rolled down the alley and shot out onto Garibaldi Avenue.

Out of sight. Though not out of earshot. Long after she disappeared from view, I could hear the rattling and grinding of her bicycle.

∽

INSIDE MORONI'S BACKROOM BAKERY, I donned my apron and grabbed a big bowl of ricotta. As I added sugar, stirring it in using a spatula, I glanced over at Angelica. As casually as I could, I asked about Liz, saying I thought I saw her on her bicycle as I was arriving.

"I gave her yesterday's bread and the cookies and pastries that we'd have to get rid of anyway," Angelica explained. "There's a food bank near us that also comes by sometimes, but I'm always glad when Liz will accept some help. I can't imagine she can do much baking in that trailer of hers."

I commented that Liz seemed quite down on her luck.

"Who knows if it's bad luck or her own choice," Angelica said. "She's either very frugal or very poor. I can't work out which it is."

I stirred the creamy ricotta filling. "How close were Liz and Mark?"

"I don't think they saw each other in recent years, unless they bumped into each other by the lake. Though, of course, before Liz's trial for killing her business partner, she and Mark saw each other every day."

I stopped stirring. "Every day? Why?"

"Why, because of Cafe Roma," Angelica said, as if she'd expected I knew. "Liz was the co-owner of the cafe. Mark was one of her business partners, too."

My jaw must have dropped, because Angelica reached out a finger and tapped my chin. "Surprised, huh?"

"A little," I admitted. "No, a lot. What happened? Why did Liz leave the cafe?"

"After she got out of prison, she gave up her stake in the cafe and moved out into the woods. Cafe Roma became Mark's. Of course, now, ironically, the cafe will go back to her."

The implications made my head spin. If Liz had once been co-owner with Mark, she might still have a key to the back door. Considering Mark never upgraded his espresso machine, it would be surprising if he bothered to pay a locksmith to change his locks after his business partner left.

Maria said she'd seen a bicycle on the day of the murder. Could it have been Liz's? I tried to recall her bicycle. Rust had eaten most of the frame, making it a brownish orange. Maria had described the bicycle as yellow. So maybe it was a different one.

Above all, I considered this: Liz stood to inherit everything. That could be a big motive for murder.

"Did Joanna ever get hold of Liz about Mark not making a will and what that means?" I asked.

"She did," Angelica said.

"How did Liz react?"

"Can you believe it? Joanna went to her trailer and found her at home. But when she told her about the inheritance, Liz slammed the door in Joanna's face."

"Why would she do that?"

"God only knows," Angelica said. Then, after picking out the crisp brown shells from the boiling oil, she added, "But maybe you'll find out. Since you're snooping around a bit."

She glanced over at me and winked.

∽

AFTER A LONG DAY OF WORK, I headed to the Old Mill for a drink, walking all the way from Garibaldi Avenue to the bar on Lake Road. Nat had insisted I come for Emma's going away party. Not that I wanted to go. Emma didn't seem to like me, and after Angelica's wink—proof she'd somehow guessed I was playing amateur sleuth—my instinct was to stay out of sight. But Nat would not take no for an answer. Nor was this murder case going to get solved from my couch.

Arriving early, I sat at the bar alone. Jerry served me a beer, and I ate slices of takeout pizza.

The Old Mill soon got busy. Emma arrived with a crowd of friends. Coming through the door, she was laughing. But when she saw me, her smile died. She narrowed her eyes and headed toward the far end of the room.

I sighed. I wished I understood how I'd offended her.

I didn't recognize most of Emma's friends. They were a younger crowd—early twenties—probably all college kids or recent graduates.

I turned my attention to my phone, taking the time to read *The Carmine Enquirer*'s latest news.

There was a story about a burger franchise in a nearby town with the headline, "*Locals fight burger joint: 'It's a stinky eyesore.'*" A photo showed one of its restaurants picketed by protesters under a big sign with its logo, a pair of massive eyes staring down at a burger. More importantly, there was a blog post about the investigation—"Carmine murder still not solved"—in which Peter criticized Chief Tedesco's lack of progress, despite the chief of police's claim to have a strong lead on a suspect (no doubt me).

The website encouraged visitors to add their email address to sign up for "breaking news alerts" delivered straight to their inbox. I signed up. Maybe Peter's snooping would turn up new information that could help me.

"I hear you got a job at Moroni's."

I looked up from my phone. Susan Davis was standing next to me, waiting for Jerry to make her a drink.

It occurred to me that Susan might know something about Mark and Liz that I hadn't already discovered. After all, she was Mark's cousin.

"Angelica saved my skin," I admitted. "What about you? How did you get your job at Parisi & Parisi?"

Susan laughed and tossed back her fake blonde curls. "Joanna came to the rescue. You probably heard that Mark fired me." She rolled her eyes. "He was always firing people. Next to saving pennies, it was his favorite thing to do."

"You must have been upset," I said.

"Nah, not really. Mark was a pain to work for—you know that—and the pay was awful. It's not like Cafe Roma was exactly a family empire. At Joanna's, I earn a lot more and the hours are good. If it weren't for my current job, I wouldn't have been able to save up to go to California."

That made sense. So much for the idea that Susan harbored any resentment toward Mark.

"I guess you'll be having a going away party soon, too," I said.

"Yeah, I can't wait. Life at home is awful. My stepfather thinks I'm a child—ever since Mom died, he's been overly protective—and still insists on a curfew. But in spring, I'm free. I'm going to the Casanova Acting Academy on a scholarship. My stepfather won't pay, and I couldn't afford the tuition on my own."

"Scholarship? That's great—I didn't realize they introduced scholarships."

"So you do know about the academy?"

My stomach did a backflip. I'd slipped up. "No, no," I spluttered. "I mean, I've heard about it. Who hasn't?"

"So true."

She gave me her best actress smile and flipped her curls over her shoulder, and it made me think she actually had a shot at being a Gold Girl. At least for a minute.

She prattled on about what a success she was going to be when she got to Hollywood, and I only half listened. I was relieved she hadn't made more of my unfortunate slip-up. And I felt sorry for her. The poor kid had no idea how tough it was to break through. She couldn't expect to show up and earn a living as an actress the next day.

"Oh, check out what one of the girls brought," Susan said excitedly, and she moved off with her drink, joining the throng of people surrounding the guest of honor.

A friend of Emma's had brought a few dress-up wigs—a purple bob, a long, straight black one, and a Marilyn Monroe lookalike—and the young women were passing them around, trying them on amidst joking and laughter.

Someone nudged me. "Any new leads, detective?"

"Hey, Nat," I said, studying his face, trying to read there what he'd meant by "detective."

He settled onto a bar stool and got straight to the point: "How come you were snooping around this morning?"

I bit my lip. How much could I tell him without revealing what I was trying to do (solve the murder) and why (because I was Eve Silver)?

"Bernie," he said with a frown. "I know you were snooping, so don't pretend you weren't."

I let out a sigh. "All right, I was snooping."

"Great." He smiled. "Now tell me, what have you found out about the murder?"

I hesitated. Then thought, *What the heck—it can't hurt to get his thoughts on it. I don't need to reveal my true identity.*

I summarized my chat with Maria last night and my encounter with Liz this morning, as well as what I'd pieced together from Anthony, Joanna, Dan, and Angelica.

"Wow," Nat said. "You've been busy. But let me get this straight. Are you suggesting Liz killed Mark to get the cafe back?"

"This is speculation. But let's assume Liz lost everything after her trial and incarceration. She retreats to the woods to live out the rest of her life in poverty. Over the years, Mark does nothing to improve the cafe. He uses cheap tricks and cuts corners. But property values have increased, making the real estate more and more valuable. He courts buyers—or maybe someone courts him—and word gets back to Liz. A deal is about to come to fruition. Maybe she resents the fortune he's sitting on. After all, it was once her cafe. Then she realizes that if he dies, she'll inherit Cafe Roma and then she can sell it and have a nice pot of money for retirement. She knows when Mark will be at work. He invites her in. She kills him. But then hears someone coming. She still has her old keys and locks the door before escaping."

"But why kill him before he sells the place? Why not wait until the deal is done? And why would she slam the door in Joanna's face when she came to tell Liz she'd inherited? It makes no sense."

Nat was right. It made no sense.

I stared into my beer, wondering what pieces of the puzzles were still missing. Part of the answer must lie in that trailer in the woods. Somehow, Liz was involved in the murder, but I couldn't see how. Not yet.

Clapping and hooting caught my attention, and I looked up.

Emma climbed onto a barstool and, from there, onto the bar itself.

She made a long rambling speech about what a welcoming bunch her friends in Carmine were and how she'd miss them in graduate school. Someone called out, "Liar," and everyone laughed, including Emma. Her demeanor was so different from the aversion she showed me. Once again, I wondered how I could have offended her.

I mentioned it to Nat.

He shrugged. "Who knows what goes on in Emma's head—least of all herself. I'm guessing that's why she's pursuing a graduate degree in psychology."

Emma was thanking her friends individually now. As

she did so, they passed the wigs around, and each time Emma called out a name, the person got a wig pulled down on her head. There was lots of laughter and clinking of glasses as the young women posed with the purple, black, and blonde wigs. Susan put on the Marilyn Monroe wig and everyone laughed, because it looked no different from her own hair.

Finally, Emma pointed her glass at Nat.

"And for Nat," she said, her tone turning serious, "who understands me better than anyone else."

Nat smiled and raised his glass to toast her. He mumbled out of the corner of his mouth, so only I could hear, "I hope that's not true…"

That was the last toast. Emma jumped off the bar, and her friends cheered. Then the party shifted into a higher gear. Voices got louder. Jerry got busier making more drinks, even lining up shot glasses on the bar. The jukebox's volume inched upward, too. Looking around, I realized the bar had become packed, and I caught glimpses of many townies: Anthony and Maria Ferrante, Joanna Parisi, and Dan Russo. Even Angelica, who stood by Dan across the bar and waved at me, a big smile on her face.

It had gotten so loud, you had to yell to be heard.

"Everyone's here," I shouted at Nat.

"Everyone," he agreed.

Behind me, a person bumped into me and laughed, and while I steadied my beer, trying not to spill, something soft land on my head, like a towel.

No, it was coarser, and it fell down the sides of my face, caressing my cheeks. I turned and saw my reflection in the mirror behind the bar, distorted by the bottles that fronted it.

I gasped. One of Emma's friends was going around

shoving the wigs on people's heads, and coming to me, she'd slipped on the blonde one. Gazing back at me from the mirror was a shockingly familiar face.

But it was Nat, staring straight at me, who named it.

"Eve Silver," he said, his eyes wide. "I knew it. You're Eve Silver."

11

"You're Eve Silver," he said again, and I ripped the wig off. For a moment, I held it in my hands, staring at it as if it was a bloody knife. Caught in the act. I threw the wig aside, turned, and bolted.

I pushed through the crowd and got to the front door and shoved it open. The humid night air swept around me as I dove down the wooden stairs to the parking lot and stumbled away. The gravel crunched underfoot, pebbles scattering. A wall of trees backed the parking lot, but they parted to make room for a path, and I hurried into the darkness, eager to disappear.

Behind me, I heard the Old Mill's front door open. The din of music and laughter from within spiked and then muffled as the door shut again. Nat called out my name.

"Bernie," he called. "Bernie, wait!"

I heard the crunch of gravel, and I floundered through the darkness, tripping over roots and stones and nearly falling.

Up ahead, in the dim light, I could make out a widening of the woods. In a clearing, a structure rose from the ground.

I stopped, panting, unsure what I was looking at, my ears filling with the sound of my breathing.

My eyes adjusted. Steps led to a raised platform covered by a wide roof. The Old Mill apparently had a music stage. It didn't provide a hiding place, though.

"Bernie."

I jumped. Nat was right behind me.

I took a step away from him.

"No, wait," he said. "Don't run away. I know why you're worried."

"Worried" didn't begin to describe it. I was scared. If my secret got out, the long, freezing winters of northern Alaska were the least of my worries. Harry Casanova would find me and then I'd be a cold corpse.

I took another step away from him.

He held out a hand, imploring me to stop.

"All right, so I know who you are. But no one else was watching you."

"They could have heard you," I said, my voice tight. A sob was lurking in my throat, threatening to jump out.

"They didn't, Bernie. It was too loud." He gave me an earnest, reassuring look. "I'm sure of it."

We watched each other for a moment.

"Now what?" I asked, as much for my own benefit as for Nat's.

"I tell no one, that's what. The world is full of crazies who hate your guts for testifying against Jay Casanova, so I understand why you don't want anyone to know. But I promise your secret is safe with me."

He took a step toward me and reached out, taking one of my hands. It sent a shock through me, but when I tried to pull away, he held on.

"I promise, Bernie. We're friends. I wouldn't do that to you."

Slowly, I nodded. Because I believed him. I believed he considered me a friend and that he would never reveal my secret. But I had to be sure.

"You swear?"

"Pinkie promise," he said.

"I'd prefer blood, but I guess pinkie will do."

He smiled. "I'm squeamish about blood, so I appreciate that."

We locked pinkie fingers, and I had a brief flashback to first grade when Tommy Reissenweber and I had made a pinkie promise to be best friends throughout elementary school. He'd kept his end of the bargain and so had I. Pinkie promises meant more to me than ink on a contract.

"Wow," Nat said, looking down at our hands, grinning. "I just made a pinkie promise with Eve Silver. Did I tell you how obsessed I was with *Silver & Gold*? I mean, like I wrote love letters to the cast and daydreamed about the show introducing a third romantic lead."

I eyed his enthusiasm with worry, biting my lip. Oh, no. It was bad enough that he knew my secret. Did he also have a crush on me—or rather on me as Eve Silver? I had to clear this up before it got complicated.

"Nat, I have to tell you..."

"That you're not attracted to me?" He laughed, evidently enjoying the surprise on my face. He seemed to be a step ahead of me. "What makes you think I'm attracted to you? I mean, in theory, I can see why some men would be interested. You're beautiful in a classic, girl-next-door kind of way. I can see why they would find you appealing. But you see, Eve Silver wasn't the one I daydreamed about kissing when I was a kid."

He smiled. I stared at him.

"Oh."

"Yeah, *oh*." He squeezed my hand and let go. "That's my small-town secret, Bernie. Not as exciting as yours, I have to say."

"Nobody knows?"

He shrugged. "Nobody asked."

"Your non-secret is safe with me."

"Until I shout it from the rooftops of the world."

"Right," I said. "Until then."

He opened his arms. He didn't need to say anything. I put my arms around him and we hugged. It not only felt good; it felt like the sealing of the pinkie promise and the admission of something that had been growing since I first met him at Cafe Roma. Nat Natale and I were real friends.

I was stepping back when the scrape of a shoe on the ground made me turn my head. A bright light flashed. I held up a hand to shield my eyes from the glare.

Emma held her phone up as a flashlight, standing where the path back to the Old Mill began. Her eyes were wide and her mouth moved, but no words came out.

Then she emitted a little squeak, like a kitten who got her tail stepped on, and she swiveled around and ran.

For a moment, Nat and I stared at the empty space she'd left behind.

"What was that about?" I asked.

"I'm afraid I understand Emma better now," Nat said, sounding weary. "That kid's got the wrong impression."

"About us?"

"About us, sure. And definitely about me."

Emma's coldness—or outright hostility—toward me suddenly made sense. She had a crush on Nat and thought I was her rival.

Nat stared into the darkness, as if trying to see Emma in the distance. "I'd better have a little chat with her."

Then he turned on his own phone's flashlight, casting a bright light on the ground and illuminating our faces. "Speaking of secrets, Bernie. I know your snooping is more than a bit of fun. You've been playing Eve Silver and trying to solve Mark's murder."

He aimed the flashlight at my face and put on a deep voice. "Do you deny it, Miss Smyth?"

I swatted away his hand. "Stop that."

"I won't stop it," he said, in his normal voice, turning off the light. "Not until you let me help."

I stared at him for a moment. If Chief Tedesco caught me investigating, I'd get into trouble, but it would be no worse than my current situation. Nat could face real repercussions, though.

"No," I said. "This gig comes with an extra sprinkling of danger."

It was a line Eve Silver herself had said in Season 2's "A Killer Crumpet." Repeating it, I felt half silly, half cool. "I can't let you do it," I added.

"Well, it's not up to you. And besides, 'If there's an extra sprinkling of danger, there's enough for two.'"

Nat winked at me. He'd repeated Adam Gold's line from the episode I'd quoted, and I couldn't help but laugh. He knew his *Silver & Gold* references.

It would be good to have a friend. Even if I could reprise my role as Eve Silver, I wasn't sure I could succeed on my own. Eve had always had a partner. Why shouldn't I?

"All right," I said, and I put a hand on Nat's shoulder. "Let's catch ourselves a killer."

12

The next morning, Friday, clouds blanketed the sky. The air was thick with humidity. As soon as I shut the door to my little house and walked down Lampedusa Lane, sweat trickled down my spine and my t-shirt stuck to my back.

Garibaldi Avenue had been closed for traffic. Already at 7 am, the setup for the festival was well underway. Booths stood ready and tents were being raised. Men and women tugged at ropes and hoisted up signs, stopping now and then to wipe the sweat from their brows.

Despite the humidity, Carmine buzzed with activity and anticipation. Even the most flushed of faces easily broke into smiles, and people laughed and joked as they worked side by side.

"Hey, *paisan*—how ya doing?"

"Tony, you awake or you still sleeping? Come help me carry this."

"Where do I leave the empty boxes?"

Half the town must have volunteered to help. Usually

deserted at this hour, Garibaldi now looked as busy as on a Saturday afternoon. Tomorrow, I imagined, the street would be packed.

Weaving in and out of the stalls, I admired the ones that were done and tried to guess what the others would turn into. One was a target practice booth. Shelves held rows of bell jars, each filled with gum balls, and for three bucks you could try to hit them with a slingshot.

As I studied the booth, I caught a flash of yellow out of the corner of my eye.

"Look out!"

Strong hands gripped me and yanked me off my feet. I fell backward with a yell of surprise and collapsed onto the sidewalk.

Something yellow sped past.

I found myself in Dan Russo's arms. He'd grabbed me, yanking me back and falling with me.

In the distance, a yellow bicycle swerved around the barriers blocking Garibaldi Avenue. The rider, wearing a hoodie that concealed their face, bent low over the racing bike. Before I could notice any more details, my attacker turned down a side street and vanished.

"Crazy," Dan said, and helped me stand.

He brushed off his khaki pants and made sure I was all right.

I heard footsteps as someone came running this way.

"You all right, Bernie?"

It was Nat. He swept his floppy hair out of his face, his eyes wide behind his round wire-frame glasses.

I nodded. "You saw what happened?"

"I saw a bicycle almost run you down and Dan pull you aside."

"Bicyclists," Dan scoffed, shaking his head. "They can be so reckless. He could have caused a terrible accident."

I glanced at Nat, and he raised an eyebrow, clearly as doubtful as I was. That bicyclist hadn't just been reckless. The rider had tried to run me down.

"Did you see who it was?" I asked Dan.

"Hoodie, sunglasses, but I didn't recognize the guy," he said. "Canary yellow bike."

"I feel I've seen that bike before."

"I have, too," Nat said, a frown on his face. "But where?"

Dan shrugged. "Maybe I have too. Whoever it is, they owe you an apology. And—" He raised a lecturing finger. "—an apology to the town. We can't have reckless driving during the street fair. Think of the headlines. First a murder, then visitors to the street fair injured by a dangerous bicyclist. A poor, innocent bystander could break their foot."

When he put it that way, it didn't sound so threatening after all.

I asked him about the street fair and whether the murder would keep people away.

"Oh, on the contrary," he said. "It seems we're likely to get more visitors than ever. Morbid curiosity makes for good business." He shrugged. "So be it. But in the Chamber of Commerce, we've also worked hard to attract as many people as we can. Angelica, Joanna, and I have invited everyone on our mailing lists and encouraged all the other businesses to do the same. I expect we'll get a lot of visitors from across the state."

A woman came by with questions about where to place a row of stands and Dan excused himself. I had to get to work, anyway. But I took a moment to stare in the bicycle's direction again.

"Why would someone want to run me down?"

"As a warning?" Nat suggested.

"A warning? You think that was the killer?"

The idea sent an icy chill down my spine and, despite the heat, goosebumps prickled my arms.

Nat had guessed I was sleuthing, and so had Angelica. Which meant the killer might have noticed, too.

I gazed off in the direction the bicyclist had vanished in. A canary yellow racing bike. A rider in a hoodie with sunglasses. A warning to stay away. But from whom?

I told Nat about my encounter with Liz Lewis on her old, rusty bike.

"Could Liz have borrowed or stolen the yellow bike?"

"It's possible, I guess," Nat said, sounding unconvinced.

I wasn't convinced either.

⁓

Above my head, the bell jingled a cheerful welcome as I stepped into Moroni's. The sign on the door had already been flipped to "Come In, We're Open," and townies occupied several tables, people no doubt involved in setting up for the street fair.

Among them sat Joanna Parisi. She was engaged in a heated conversation with three women and two men at nearby tables, all of them drinking coffee and eating Angelica's pastries.

"Everyone knows the case hinged on that woman's testimony," one patron said, her voice rising to an angry pitch. "If she lied..."

Joanna shook her head. "If she lied, the DEA evidence would have landed Jay Casanova in jail, anyway."

The angry woman crossed her arms and scowled. "Jay is innocent. I know it in my heart."

My own heart sank. The last thing I wanted to hear about was Jay Casanova, his trial, and how I supposedly had perjured myself to destroy an innocent man.

Joanna saw me standing by the entrance and smiled at me. "What about you, Bernie? Do you think Jay Casanova was guilty?"

How could people still ask this question, even after that long trial? Roberta LaRosa's claim that the tide was turning, and most had changed their minds and now saw Jay as a crook, was encouraging. As for myself, I had never doubted his guilt, not after what I discovered that day on the set of *Silver & Gold*.

We were shooting on location in Durango, Mexico, by an old abandoned warehouse. Since *Silver & Gold* had begun using Casanova Enterprises' crew, we'd been shooting on location a lot in Mexico, supposedly because it was cheap and, as Jay said, it gave the show an "edgy and exotic" quality. Like his movies.

But while I was on the set, I noticed we had a couple more trucks than we usually needed for our equipment. One in particular made me curious, because the crew never opened it to get gear.

On the last morning of the shoot, I arrived early to the shoot and noticed the back of the extra grip truck stood ajar. Inside, I found what I'd expect to find. Cameras. Boom poles. Boxes full of neatly coiled cables. Everything looked normal.

Until I sniffed the air. The truck smelled of coffee. That was strange. Guess some guys were bringing back a few crates of coffee.

At the very back of the truck, they had stacked a wall of unmarked boxes. I pulled one out, and finding a box cutter, cut it open. The box was full of coffee beans. I cut open another box, and it revealed more coffee beans.

Strange thing for Casanova Enterprises to be transporting. As far as I knew, Jay didn't have a sideline in coffee.

Then I dug my hands into the coffee beans.

Buried within were bags of cocaine.

I sealed the boxes and closed the truck and walked away. But before we returned to the U.S., I made a call.

The DEA stopped the trucks on the U.S. side of the border and they traced the cocaine shipment back to Jay. It turned out he was using film shoots south of the border to smuggle drugs into the U.S. and guns back to Mexico.

In the weeks after that, I helped the DEA get access to Jay's business files, and even wore a wire while talking to him about "special business opportunities" down south. By the time they arrested Jay, the DEA had an airtight case.

The big question in the media was, of course, "why?" Jay was rich, successful, beloved by millions. But apparently fame and fortune as a Hollywood star wasn't enough. He wanted more. Always more, more, and more. He wanted—in his own words—to build an empire. Fast.

What he got was a lifetime in prison.

So, did I believe Jay Casanova was guilty? Of course I did. I knew he was guilty.

What I told Joanna was this: "I guess if a judge and jury convicted him, there must be some truth to the matter."

The angry woman huffed.

Joanna nodded. "I agree. This isn't a case where the justice system got it wrong. Though, of course, some people disagree with us, Bernie."

She glanced toward the angry Jay lover, and then rolled her eyes at me, making clear just what she thought of the woman.

My heart lifted, and I smiled. It was good to know that people believed me—even if they didn't know my true identity.

~

My first job this morning was quality testing, tasting the three kinds of cannoli we'd be selling at tomorrow's fair: chocolate chips, chopped pistachios, and candied fruit.

I chose a chocolate-chip cannoli from the tray in the bakery and bit into it, closing my eyes as I made a deep "mmm" sound.

"What's the secret, Angelica? Even the chocolate chips taste unlike any other chocolate chips I've ever had."

"The trick is to buy high-quality dark chocolate—at least 70% cocoa—and then chop it yourself. Store-bought chips are never as good."

Though I agreed, store-bought chips would have made our jobs easier. Between today and tomorrow's street fair, we would need to make 300 cannolis.

As we worked, I reflected on Angelica's approach to baking. Every choice she made "favored the flavor," as she herself said. No shortcuts. No cheap ingredients. In contrast, Mark had stood for cheapness.

Angelica's baked goods and coffees cost more than Mark's had. In fact, they cost more than other mainstream cafes, yet by staying true to her vision, she'd attracted the right kinds of customers from all over the state.

Mark had lacked that kind of vision, and it was interesting what Maria had said—that he'd considered the cafe a burden. No doubt he was looking forward to selling it. But what were his plans for afterward? He was too young to retire. Even if Dan was right and the the cafe sale would yield a lot of money, it couldn't be enough for the rest of Mark's life, not even in the relatively affordable town of Carmine. Mark had lived above the cafe—where had he planned to live once he'd sold the building?

These thoughts carried me through the early morning—occasionally interrupted by customers coming into the bakery—until Angelica and I had made a big batch of cannolis.

"Can you bring a tray over to Carlo's for me?" she asked, as I added the last tray to the wheeled rack behind the counter. "He'll need them for the lunch crowd, and they'll be ordering sweet stuff within the hour."

I grabbed a tray with the three types of cannoli and slid it off the rack. I made my way out of Moroni's. The bakery was getting busy, and I promised Angelica I'd be right back.

Outside it was getting hot, and I hurried to the restaurant, afraid the ricotta cream and the chocolate would melt before I could deliver the goods to Carlo.

As I eased open the door to Carlo's and stepped inside, he called out my name.

"Bernie, what excellent timing."

He seemed excited about something as he took the tray from me, and I sensed it wasn't the cannoli.

"I've seen him," he said. "Our mystery man."

I looked around, my stomach doing a little pirouette. "Where? When?"

"I saw him in the street. Maybe he got here early to check out the fair before it starts. He passed the window only ten minutes ago. Didn't he, Maria? You saw the mystery man, too, didn't you?"

Maria was standing at the bar, polishing wine glasses. "I did. Only I don't think he's such a mystery."

I raised an eyebrow, waiting for her to elaborate.

"He can't be a mystery," she said. "Not when he's Mark's cousin."

13

I bolted out of Carlo's, scanning the crowd in the street.

Maria had described Mark's cousin as tall, handsome, with black hair. Gray suit pants and a light-blue button-down shirt.

People crowded the street. A welter of volunteers carried boxes and strung cables and hung decorations. I caught a flash of blue, but it was a woman in a t-shirt tacking an "I Love Italy" poster to the side of a stall.

I moved down into the street and, weaving in and out of the stands, studied the faces and hairdos.

Plenty of black hair, but tall and handsome?

I sighed. The guy was probably long gone.

I turned to go back to Moroni's, and then saw him. Gray suit pants and a light-blue button-down shirt. He was two blocks away, walking along the sidewalk with his hands in his pockets.

I broke into a run. "Hey, you," I called out.

I ran down the middle of Garibaldi Avenue, ducked between two stalls, and hit the sidewalk on the same side as the mystery man.

No, no longer a mystery. Mark's cousin.

I called out again to make him stop.

This time he turned.

When he saw me running toward him, his eyes widened. He yanked his hands out of his pockets. Turning around again, he strode off, increasing his pace. His long legs carried him quickly down the sidewalk, but I was gaining on him. He glanced back and increased his speed.

Another set of barriers at this end of Garibaldi also kept traffic out. Beyond them, he stopped at a Lexus parked in front of the municipal building. He pulled the keys out of his pocket, fumbling with them before opening the driver's door.

He ducked into the seat. As I came to the car, the door was still open.

"I need to talk to you," I said.

"I have nothing to say," he said, frowning. "I don't want trouble. Leave me alone."

Before I could wedge myself in the door, he slammed it, and I nearly got my fingers caught. I grabbed the door handle and yanked, but he'd locked it.

Giving me a hard glare through the window, he started the engine.

An instant later, he pulled out and hit the gas, sending his car flying forward.

I watched the Lexus speed up Garibaldi and then turn and zoom up Cedar Hill, disappearing from sight.

I stomped my foot and cursed myself.

"Should've kept your big mouth shut."

I'd warned him I was coming. If I hadn't shouted at him, I might have crept up and cornered him. Now I'd scared him off—maybe for good.

∽

I wandered back toward Moroni's, hands in my pockets, eyes on my feet, thinking of the dozen things I should have done—but didn't do—to catch the mystery man. I wasn't looking and walked right into another person on the sidewalk.

"Oh, sorry," I said.

Susan laughed. "Look where you're going, clumsy."

She was standing outside Parisi & Parisi's offices, holding a brown paper bag and a metal canteen.

"I'm heading up to the Overlook for my lunch break," she explained.

It suddenly occurred to me that if Maria was right and the mystery man was Mark's cousin, then Susan might know him. After all, she was Mark's cousin, too.

"Susan," I said. "Just the person I wanted to talk to."

I explained what Carlo and Maria had told me and how I'd chased down Mark's cousin.

Susan frowned. "But why would he come back? Liz will inherit. There's nothing for him here."

There was a note of displeasure in her voice, as if she didn't like the idea of the guy coming around.

"Who is he?" I asked.

"His name's Steve something. I don't really know that side of the family. I only know that he's considered a bad apple. Mark didn't like him. And now he's creeping around Carmine? I bet it's because he's hoping to get a piece of the pie."

I shook my head. "But what would he inherit, if he's not named in a will?"

"Nothing. See, here's what Joanna explained to me. Liz is

the closest next of kin. She stands to inherit everything. Unless..." Susan looked thoughtful.

I suddenly remembered what Joanna had explained about the 120-hour rule in New Jersey.

"If Liz inherits and then dies later," I said, "everything she inherited from Mark is hers. And she can pass that down to her relatives. But if Liz dies within 120 hours of Mark's death, then the succession goes to Mark's next relative in line."

"That's right," Susan said, eyeing me with surprise. "How did you know that? Oh, wait. Joanna must have told you, too."

I nodded. "The point being that if Liz died today—before the 120 hours run out tomorrow morning—Mark's cousin would inherit, wouldn't he?"

"Sure," Susan said, and then shrugged. "But so would I. Mark has two cousins, one from each side of the family." She laughed. "But come on, you're not actually thinking this burglar will somehow strike again and kill Liz, too? What are the chances of that?"

My limbs had turned to stone. All this time, I'd suspected Liz, because she would inherit, but what if the killer wasn't done removing obstacles to his inheritance?

Steve had turned up Cedar Hill, which led to Lake Road. What if he was looking for Liz? What if he intended to kill her?

Liz might be in mortal danger.

14

Even as I ran across the street to Moroni's, I had my phone in my hand, pressed to my ear, murmuring, "Come on, Nat, pick up, pick up..."

Finally, he picked up. I didn't give him a chance to speak. As I pushed my way through the jangling door to the bakery, I spilled out the details under my breath.

"I'm on board," he said. "I'll be waiting in my car outside the public library—on the other side of the street fair barriers."

I hung up and pocketed my phone.

A single customer stood by the counter, an elderly gentleman in a neat suit and tie, who was studying the cookies with the seriousness of a scholar.

I slipped around him and came face to face with Angelica. I grabbed both her hands and looked her in the eye.

"Angelica, listen..."

She at once saw that something serious had happened. "Sweetie, what's wrong?"

How much could I tell her? She'd already guessed I was snooping around, but it was different to admit openly that I was chasing Mark's killer. I loved Angelica, but she might worry, or even worse, tell someone else, like Joanna, who would only spread the gossip to the rest of town. If I was wrong about Mark's cousin, it would put the killer on guard.

"An urgent thing has come up," I said. "Urgently."

"An urgent thing urgently?"

"Can I take an extended lunch break?"

I bit my lip. How much did her look of concern have to do with how busy the bakery was at this time of day? Not to mention the 300 cannolis.

"Of course, *mia cara,*" she said. She squeezed my hands. "But be careful."

With a quick "thanks," I spun around and flung open the door to the bakery—the bell protested, jingling more dramatically than usual—and I bolted down the sidewalk, heading toward the public library.

All around me, people were still busy setting up the stands for the street fair, and I had to dodge two men carrying a giant popcorn machine.

As promised, Nat had parked by the curb in front of the public library. In front of a fire hydrant, of all places. It would be our luck for Chief Tedesco to appear now and arrest me for public endangerment because of blocking a fire hydrant.

I jumped into the car. Nat drove an old Honda Accord with dancing bear stickers on the back and a pair of tie-dye dice hanging from the rearview mirror. He revved the engine—maybe with more enthusiasm than was strictly necessary—and the car flung me back in my seat as we shot forward.

He swerved up Cedar Hill with a screech of tires. The engine growled unhappily. I gave him a raised eyebrow, and he responded with a grin. "When am I ever going to be in a car chase again?"

"Let's hope it is a car chase," I said, "and not the discovery of a new body."

That put a damper on Nat's spirits, and he drove less recklessly. His Honda chugged up the steep road over Cedar Hill, past all the fancy Victorian mansions.

Even as we crested the hill, my thoughts lingered with Angelica and the mountain of cannoli we had to prepare for tomorrow. My chest tightened. I'd left her in the lurch. I silently promised myself—and her—that I would make it up to her. I'd give 110 percent this afternoon and tomorrow morning. Moroni's would shine at the street fair, and Angelica would win the cannoli competition. I would see to it.

Nat steered the car along the winding Lake Road, trees whizzing past us.

"By the way, I talked to Emma," Nat said. "I'd never seen her blush so much. She kept saying, 'I'm such an idiot, I'm such an idiot.' Though honestly, how was she supposed to know? It's not like I go around town with a t-shirt on saying, 'Hi, I'm Nat, I'm gay.' Well, I told her that and she kept shaking her head and saying, 'No, it's not just that. I can't believe what I've done. I'm such an idiot.'" He gave a little shrug. "She'll get over it, though."

I nodded. I was glad he'd squared things with Emma, but my mind was on Liz. What if we arrived too late?

"Bernie," Nat said, and I heard caution in his voice. "You haven't called the cops, have you?"

I shook my head.

"We can't do this alone. Not if Mark's cousin really is the killer."

I looked at my phone and sighed. He was right, of

course. I didn't trust Chief Tedesco, though, and how would I explain all this to her, anyway? She'd only find some excuse to turn it into an accusation—more proof that I was at fault.

Nat must have interpreted my hesitation as resistance, because he said, "Bernie, we need to call the cops."

"All right," I said,

I got Anthony's number from Nat and hit dial. After a couple of rings, he answered.

"Bernie," he said, sounding happy to hear from me.

I cut to the chase: "I'm worried Mark's killer may strike again."

His tone turned serious. "Tell me what you know."

I filled him in on what I knew about Mark's cousin, Steve, and how he'd rushed off when I tried to talk to him. And what—between Joanna and Susan—I understood about the 120-hour rule: The cousins stood next in line to inherit, but only if Liz died before the morning.

"We're on our way to the lake now," I said.

"Leave this to me," Anthony said. "It may be dangerous. Don't go to the lake, Bernie."

I blew air through my teeth, making a shushing noise, and I said, "Sorry, Anthony. The connection is bad."

More shushing.

"What was that? What did you say?"

Then I hung up.

A moment later, my phone rang. Anthony's number. I rejected the call.

Nat gave me a raised eyebrow. "That was subtle."

"Anthony won't get there before us, and we may already be too late. Liz's life may depend on us acting quickly."

"Aye, aye, captain."

Nat floored the accelerator.

∽

THE TIRES on the car bit into the gravel, kicking up pebbles, as Nat swerved into the parking lot by the boathouse.

"And you accused me of not being subtle," I said.

But I appreciated the urgency, and as soon as we came to a standstill, I jumped out of the car.

Nat got out, too.

Looking around, I saw no other cars in the lot, which was odd.

"You stay here," I said.

"No way," Nat protested. "We go together."

"If this guy, Steve, comes back this way, you'll need to either stop him or chase him."

Nat stared at me for a moment, then swept his bangs aside, as if getting ready. "All right. I'll be on guard. But don't be a hero."

"I won't."

He wished me luck, and I wished him luck, and then I turned and jogged past the boathouse and down into the soft sand.

Next to trudging through mud, running through sand comes closest to the experience of a nightmare during waking hours. You run and run—really lean into it—but you seem to go no faster.

It was driving me crazy, until I remembered I could run in the shallows, where the sand was harder, and I made better time.

Soon I was climbing the path into the woods.

Roots criss-crossed the trail, and I had to be careful not to twist an ankle. In *Silver & Gold*, Eve Silver ran through pitch-black warehouses, sprinted through dense woods, and even chased a crook across a recently plowed field. And yet she never twisted an ankle. I knew by now that I didn't quite have Eve's luck or superhuman abilities, so I slowed down to pick my way across the roots.

I caught sight of Liz's trailer and stopped.

All was quiet. I saw no sight of anyone outside, though Liz's canoe lay bottom up on the ground and her rusty bike leaned against the trailer. Was she home? Was she still alive?

I crept closer, weaving from tree to tree, trying to stay as hidden as possible.

Was someone peering out from within the trailer? I couldn't tell. The long, narrow window to the left of the door had curtains, but they didn't move.

I hid behind a tree about twelve feet from the trailer. I waited a moment, trying to listen past the thud-thud-thud of my heart.

Branches creaked. A bird called out. But otherwise, I heard nothing unusual.

I crouched down and ran to the trailer. I flattened my back against it and waited. My heart increased its dull drilling in my ears, which made it difficult to tell—was that the sound of movement from within?

I didn't think so.

I reached out and grabbed the door handle. Probably locked.

I pressed down, and it clicked open. Nope, not locked.

I swung the door open, expecting Steve to come barreling out, a crazed grin on his face, butcher knife raised above his head...

When nothing happened, I peered inside. Then took a deep breath and stepped through the door.

The trailer was empty.

I stepped all the way inside, allowing the door to swing shut behind me.

The trailer bore the marks of a simple life. A fishing pole rested in a corner by an eating nook. Its tiny formica table offered room for only two people. Between the table and a narrow door (presumably to a toilet), the appliances stood embedded in the wall: a fridge below, a minuscule stovetop and counter in the middle, and a microwave up above.

At the back, a raised platform contained a bed—a small double with a single sheet and pillow. Apart from this, there was a narrow counter with a row of books with a knife block serving as a bookend closest to the door I'd come through.

I wrinkled my nose: a whiff of mildew and something chemical. Maybe bug spray.

Stepping further inside, I glanced at the books, at first thinking nothing of them. Then I looked again.

Walden by Henry David Thoreau. Also, *The Maine Woods. The SAS Survival Guide: How to Survive in the Wild, on Land or Sea*. There were books with the writings of Marcus Aurelius, Seneca, and Thich Nhat Hanh. And finally, at the end of the row, nearest the bedroom, a book I had seen recently:

A Moron's Step-by-Step Guide to Living with Less.

It was the book Mark had been reading. The one Anthony had said was missing. Seeing it in Liz's trailer jolted me.

What did it mean? Had Liz and Mark been closer than I first thought? What was in this book that could have unified these two ex-business partners? Or had Liz stolen Mark's copy?

I flipped it open and noticed how many passages had been underlined. The margins were thick with scrawled comments. I looked closely at the front. It was wrinkled but intact—this couldn't be Mark's book. That one had a torn cover.

The linoleum floor creaked behind me.

I spun around.

Liz Lewis stood five feet from me. Somehow, she'd opened the door and crept into the trailer without my noticing. Now she held a knife from the block. It was a carving knife, and its long blade looked sharp.

Her hand was steady as she aimed the blade at me, her eyes fierce and cold.

"You're snooping around the wrong place, missy."

15

Liz pointed the knife blade at me.

I staggered backward, my shoe hitting a low step. Behind me, the platform rose to the nook with the bed. To my left was the narrow door to the toilet and to the right, the books. Liz blocked the trailer's only exit.

My mind raced. Had my earlier suspicions about Liz been correct after all? I considered the knife in Mark's back, the knife she'd used to stab her other business partner, the knife she was holding now. Would she attack me?

I took a deep breath and held up my hands.

"I'm sorry for sneaking into your home," I said. "I meant no harm."

She glared at me, but said nothing.

"I meant to find you and warn you," I went on. "Your life may be in danger."

As quickly and succinctly as I could, I summarized what had happened with the mystery man—Mark's cousin—and how I believed he might intend to kill Liz for the inheritance.

She snorted. "What is this, one of Mark's cousins on his

mom's side of the family? I don't know diddly-squat about the extended family, nor do I care. Besides, if this cousin of Mark's—"

"Steve," I said.

"Steve," she repeated with a grimace, as if the name itself offended her. "Well, if this Steve wanted to kill me, why hasn't he tried to already?"

I thought about that. "Maybe he tried to find you, but he doesn't live in Carmine, so he couldn't rely on bumping into you, and even locals like Joanna have a hard time locating you."

Again, she snorted. "I'm out most days, but I sleep here every night. All this killer cousin would need to do is drive over at night and attack me. I don't buy it."

But at least by now she'd lowered the knife. I reached out a hand.

"Why don't you give me the knife and we can talk this through? My only concern is making sure that you're safe and that Mark's killer is caught. We both want that, don't we?"

She gave me a hard look, then shrugged and turned the knife handle toward me. With relief, I grasped the knife and put it down on the counter by the books.

"I assumed you'd come snooping because you thought I killed Mark," Liz said, eyeing me suspiciously.

Her accusation took me aback. She must have seen my surprise, because slowly, her glare turned to a smirk. "That's right, missy, I'm no idiot. When Joanna told me I was next of kin and then Anthony Ferrante stopped by to question me, I put two and two together. You're not the only person in town who thought, 'Hey, that crazy lady in the woods—it must be her.' Am I right?"

I rubbed the back of my neck, embarrassed. "All right, guilty as charged. I did suspect you."

"Ha, I knew it." She seemed pleased by my admission. "Because you thought I needed the money?"

I nodded.

"I don't need Mark's money, and I have no interest in it. Money never brought me anything but misery."

I kept quiet, letting her speak, and she gazed off into the middle distance.

"I was a successful businesswoman…"

Slowly, her story emerged.

Liz had not only co-owned Cafe Roma, she'd also been the landlady for several commercial tenants in the area. On top of which, she ran a company with a business partner—a mail order service selling DIY tools and supplies. When the internet came along, the business boomed and made them millions. Liz moved into the most enviable old Victorian mansion on Cedar Hill.

"But I was miserable," she said. "My business partner and I squabbled over money. Joe was a greedy man, almost as greedy as I was, and he claimed the mail order concept had been his idea. He demanded more profits. One day, our fight turned violent. Joe tried to stab me. I grabbed a kitchen knife and fought him. You probably know the rest of that story from town gossip."

I nodded.

"Well, once in prison, I read a lot of books. As a kid, I'd loved Thoreau's *Walden*, and as a businesswoman I saw his philosophy of self-reliance as a kind of intellectual lodestar."

I too had loved *Walden* when I was a kid, and I'd even attempted to spend one year of middle school in the tree house in my backyard, only to discover that my addiction to

TV trumped my back-to-nature ambitions. In the end, I lasted one night before returning to the house, tail between my legs.

Liz continued her story. "But when I reread the book, I saw it with fresh eyes. My idea of self-reliance, I realized, was a load of bull. Owning property. Running a big business. All fueled by greed. What kind of self-reliance was that? *Walden* led me to Emerson, which led to the classics—Plato, Seneca, and so on. By the time I read *A Moron's Step-by-Step Guide to Living with Less*, a plan was forming in my mind. I knew what to do. When I got out of prison, I sold the house and what remained of my businesses, and I bought a trailer and a plot of land in the woods. My bank account is stuffed to the gills with money, but I don't plan on using it. Knowing it sits there is a constant reminder of my accomplishment. As Thoreau said, 'A man is rich in proportion to the number of things which he can afford to let alone.'"

Her eyes glistened, her face lighting up with a kind of religious fervor.

"I'm glad to hear you're happy now," I said.

Her smile dried up. She frowned, and she fixed me with a glare, the spell broken. "Who the hell said anything about being happy?"

"What about Mark?" I asked. "Was he happy?"

"Miserable bastard wouldn't know happiness if it chewed his leg off."

Obviously, Liz and Mark shared some DNA. If there was a grumpy gene, they both got it.

"What about this book?" I pointed to *A Moron's Step-by-Step Guide to Living with Less*. "I saw Mark reading it. Did he get it from you?"

"I recommended it, yes," she said. "We bumped into each other at the boathouse and he was complaining about the cafe. He was always complaining about the cafe. I told him what I thought of his moaning. 'If you want to change things, Mark, you're the only one who can do it. Sell up, get rid of everything, and embrace a minimalist lifestyle, where you're not dependent on other people.'"

She smiled grimly, crossing her arms.

"You inspired him," I said.

"Call it what you will. He saw the results of my freedom. I've cut ties with all you idiots. I told Mark he could do it too. And let me tell you, it was a hoot to watch him inch his way toward liberty. I couldn't wait to see the shock on people's faces when they learned what he'd planned."

Not only did Liz not have a motive for killing Mark for his money, she seemed to take pleasure in watching him dispense with his earthly goods. She probably wouldn't have cared too much if he'd failed to go through with his plans—it wasn't likely they would have wound up living happily ever after in a trailer together—but she'd seen the light and no doubt enjoyed proselytizing to her nephew.

His frugality made more sense now. He didn't care about the business in the long term. Disappoint a customer? No problem. Hire a barista to do the work he hated? Makes sense. Skimp on coffee so he'd spend less of his cash on the business? Sure.

All along, Mark had been inching his way toward "living with less."

Something occurred to me. "If Steve wanted Mark's money, why not wait until after the cafe was sold? Then he'd inherit cash, not a property that he'd have to sell."

"Because there would be no money left to inherit."

Liz picked up the book—*A Moron's Step-by-Step Guide to Living with Less*—and flipped through the pages. When she'd found what she was looking for, she shoved the book at me.

I read the page heading.

"'Chapter 7. Giving it all away to charity.'"

I looked up at Liz. "He was going to get rid of everything?"

She chuckled. "The whole kit and caboodle."

~

My walk back to the boathouse was slow. I dragged my feet across the root-choked path, studying the ground as I thought things over.

By tomorrow morning, Mark's assets would fully transfer to Liz. Then she'd be safe.

Until then, she was in danger. Steve could attack at any moment. She ought to contact the police and get help. But she'd snorted, dismissing my suggestion. She claimed she could handle an aggressive man—she'd done it before.

She'd been cagey about what she would do with Mark's money, and when I asked her outright whether she would donate the inheritance to a charity, as her nephew had intended, she snapped at me: "My money, my business."

Something told me she was going to sell the cafe and deposit the proceeds in her bank account with the rest of her wealth. And let it sit. Maybe Liz Lewis, hoarding all her money, wasn't as unburdened from material life as she'd like to think.

As she said, it was none of my business.

What mattered was that Mark must have told others about his plans. Steve somehow found out—at the lunch at Carlo's, maybe—and realized that if he didn't strike now, he'd never have the chance to get the money he wanted.

I walked across the sand beach, trying to imagine Steve.

I'd caught only a brief glimpse of him getting into his car and he'd looked like a million other suburban businessmen.

I knew too little about Steve. Which meant I was in the dark about what his next move would be. If only Liz wouldn't be so stubborn and accept protection from the police.

With that thought in my mind, it was a relief to see Anthony Ferrante stepping out of his patrol car. Nat leaned against his own car, parked next to Anthony's, and they both looked at me expectantly as I approached.

"I just got here," Anthony said. "Is everything all right?"

"Liz is all right," I confirmed. "But she refuses help and Steve is still on the loose."

Anthony frowned. "You'd better tell me everything you know."

I took a deep breath and let out a sigh. Whatever I told him would get back to Chief Tedesco. Any pretense that I wasn't sleuthing would be pointless, but if I were to choose between keeping my secret and saving Liz's life, I knew there was no choice at all: I had to make sure Liz stayed safe.

"Let's go back to the morning I found Mark," I said.

I described the signs I'd seen that Mark had a visitor before I arrived and how that had led me to Liz at first, only to prove a false lead as Steve came into the picture. I ended on the revelation that Mark had intended to give away all his assets and retreat to a life in the woods, like Liz.

Anthony shook his head and gave me a stern look. "You should have come to the police with this information much sooner."

It was my turn to look stern. "And what would that have gotten me? Your chief is trying to pin this murder on me, and there's nothing I can say that will make her change her mind."

Anthony scratched his chin. "Well, yeah, you've got a point. But you could have come to me."

"I just did, Anthony," I said, still miffed that I was being scolded for not cooperating with the police.

In part, because he was right. I really should have.

Anthony opened his mouth to say something when his radio crackled to life. The dispatcher started with a call sign and then let off a volley of codes and words.

"Repeat, possible crime in progress."

Anthony grabbed his radio and responded while Nat and I stood frozen side by side. I couldn't catch all the words, but it was clear something serious had happened.

Anthony jumped into his seat and shut the door and grabbed the wheel.

"There's been an attack," he said through the open window, his tires already throwing up gravel as he backed up and turned the car.

His last words out the window made my gut tighten into a tiny ball.

"An attack at the Overlook."

Then he sped off.

Nat and I looked at each other, and I cursed myself. Susan had gone to the Overlook. If Steve wanted all the money to himself, Liz wasn't his only target.

I'd rushed to protect the wrong person.

16

"I should have stopped Susan from going to the Overlook," I said for the tenth time.

Nat squeezed my hand. "You couldn't have known."

But that was what bothered me. I should have known. Now that we were sitting at Moroni's, each with a giant cup of latte in front of us, courtesy of Angelica, the danger to Susan seemed so blatantly obvious that I felt ashamed of myself. Eve Silver would have caught the whiff of danger from a mile away. I had been standing next to Susan before she left for her lunch break and all I could think of was Liz. Without a script, this sleuthing stuff was hard.

Angelica swept over to our table with a plate of pizzelle —delicious, crunchy waffle cookies, with a hint of anise.

"Eat, drink," she ordered, and hurried back to the counter to serve the steady stream of customers.

Once she learned what had happened, she'd refused my offer to help and insisted I sit down.

I took a sip of my coffee. The steamed milk made the

coffee taste as rich as hot chocolate. I closed my eyes, savoring it.

When I opened them, Nat was staring at me.

"You all right?"

I shrugged. "I'm not the one in danger. If only I could call Liz to make sure she was all right."

"She doesn't have a phone."

"Then I wish we could know whether Susan is alive or—"

I choked on the last word, suddenly feeling the day—and the past few days—bear down on me. Mark had been killed on Tuesday. Today was Friday. Yet it felt like an eternity had passed.

"Tomorrow is Saturday," I mumbled to myself. Then, remembering the silent promise I'd made to Angelica, my heart skipped a beat. "Oh, no. Tomorrow's Saturday. Angelica needs to be ready for tomorrow's cannoli competition, and I've done nothing to help her."

"You've done plenty," Angelica said.

She'd finished with the last customer and came to retrieve our empty cups and plates.

"I'll handle the dishes," I insisted, and when Angelica protested in her motherly way, I added, "I'm better off working than stewing on all the things I should have done and didn't do."

Nat explained he'd better get back to work, too. A moment later, he was gone, and I was wearing an apron and standing at the worktable in the kitchen, filling cannoli shells with ricotta cream for the big day tomorrow.

My attempts to stay entirely focused on the present moment and the task at hand proved difficult—I reached for a spatula and saw a knife nearby and shuddered.

Where is Steve? Is Susan all right?

Caught in a trance of cannoli making, I lost track of time. When I heard Anthony's voice up front, I snapped out of my daydream, quickly washed my hands and wiped them off, and hurried to the front counter.

"Anthony," I exclaimed.

He was standing by the cash register and so was Angelica, who was looking worried, but he gave me a smile when she saw me.

"She's alive," Angelica said, clasping her hands together. "Susan's alive."

"Is she all right?" I asked Anthony.

"She's at the hospital," he said. "After a long search, we found her in the woods, half a mile from the Overlook. Despite the shock, she's been able to tell us everything. Her attacker ambushed her on the trail and she ran. When he caught up with her, she fought him off, but she sustained several knife wounds. Nothing life threatening, though. She'll recover."

I was so relieved I nearly cried. Angelica, seeing my face, took a step toward me and put an arm around my shoulder.

"Did you catch him?" I asked Anthony.

He shook his head, a grim look on his face. "The perp is still at large, and although Susan thinks it was a man, the person wore a ski mask. So we don't have a detailed description. But we're keeping an eye out for the Lexus you saw, and based on your description of this guy, Steve, we at least have a good lead. Assuming he is the one who attacked Susan."

"What about Liz?" I asked.

"We've posted a patrol car by the boathouse and a pair of officers will remain on guard around the clock."

I wondered how much Liz would dislike that—a lot, I

suspected—and imagined she'd take off in her canoe at the first opportunity she had. But it reassured me the cops were taking the threat seriously.

Anthony's radio crackled and the dispatcher spoke.

"There's been some development—I have to head back to the station." Anthony gave me a nod, his expression serious. "I thought you'd like to hear Susan's alive."

"Thanks, Anthony."

After he left the bakery, I stared at the door for a moment. Angelica did, too. Then she undid my apron on the back and slipped it over my head.

"What are you doing?" I asked, surprised.

"I'm getting back to work," she said. "But you, Bernie, are going to the hospital to visit Susan."

We looked at each other for a moment. She'd known what I wanted to do even before I could articulate it to myself. I threw my arms around her and gave her a long hug. She held me. When we separated, she touched my cheek. "You've got important work to do, sweetie, and it's not making cream for cannolis. Not right now."

∼

A POLICE OFFICER, sitting on a chair and reading a glossy travel magazine, guarded the door to Susan's room on the third floor of the hospital. He looked up.

"You can visit for five minutes," he said. "But the door stays open."

Susan lay propped up in bed, thin tubes coming out of heavily bandaged arms. When she saw Nat and me coming through the door, she smiled weakly.

"It's so good of you to come," she said.

"The nurse said you're going to recover," I said.

"I won't even have permanent scars—thank God." She gazed upward and made the sign of the cross, tugging at the tubes. "I can't believe how lucky I was."

Nat laughed. "Even after a killer attacks you, you're worried about how you look."

"An actress is half talent, half good looks."

I shuddered. Jay Casanova used to say that. It summed up his casting philosophy. If Susan had taken such maxims to heart, she really would make a good Gold Girl, or whatever replaced the concept now that Jay was in prison.

"Anthony Ferrante told me you fought off the attacker," I said. "That was very brave."

Susan gave a little shrug. "I didn't feel brave. I felt terrified."

She told us what she'd told the cops: she'd taken the forest trail to the Overlook to eat her lunch when a man in a ski mask had jumped out.

"He said nothing, but I'm pretty sure it was a man, and I'm pretty sure it was Mark's cousin. He had a knife, and he slashed at me. I screamed. Of course, with my bad luck, there was no one else out in the woods. So I turned and ran. He caught up with me, and then, desperate, I grabbed a broken branch off the ground and fought him. He cut me, but I clubbed him across the head and he staggered off. I called 911, but my phone battery was low and it died while I spoke with the emergency dispatcher. I wandered in the woods for a while, hiding behind trees every time I heard a sound, afraid the guy was coming back. Finally, the cops found me."

I thought for a moment. "Any idea how he knew you'd be at the Overlook?"

Susan shook her head. "Maybe he followed me."

"It is interesting that he'd attack you," I said. Then thought better of the word choice. "Uh, horrific, nightmarish, I mean. But also unexpected. Why not attack Liz first?"

"Maybe it was too obvious," Susan suggested.

Nat nodded. "You spotted him in town, Bernie, and chased him off. Then we turned up at Liz's trailer, followed by Anthony. Maybe Steve was spying on us. The police cruiser might have rattled him, and he changed his plans."

"I guess that makes sense."

Still, I couldn't help but feel I was missing some crucial detail. Steve, if he was the killer, knew more than we did, and yet his attack on Susan seemed so desperate.

"Mark's murder wasn't exactly smoothly executed," Susan said, when I shared my thoughts. "In Cafe Roma, Steve probably got interrupted and had to run off, so he set the body on fire to cover his tracks. When he attacked me in the woods, it wasn't a well-rehearsed ambush. Maybe he'd planned to hit Liz, then saw Anthony hanging around, so he decided to get rid of me instead. He would have to get rid of me sooner or later, anyway."

I nodded. "That's true."

"But he's pushed his luck," Susan said. "The cops will catch him now."

I hoped she was right. I gave her a reassuring smile and gently squeezed her hand, wanting her to feel comforted by the idea that the cops would catch her attacker soon.

The police officer guarding the door told us our five minutes were up.

As Nat and I walked out of the room, he asked me, "You don't look convinced. You don't think they're going to catch him any time soon, do you?"

I was quiet for a while. We stepped into the elevator, and I pressed the button for the lobby. "Either Steve is insane or he's incredibly confident. Maybe both. Once he's removed the obstacles to his inheritance, how does he expect to collect the money? The cops know he's the killer." I shook my head. "I worry he's got a trick up his sleeve."

"Maybe it's like Susan says, he's not as smooth as he'd like to be. Maybe he's desperate. Why else kill in the first place?"

"Either way, for as long as he's on the loose, he's a threat to both Susan and Liz," I said. "I just hope the police can keep a close watch on Liz…"

The elevator doors opened, and as we stepped into the lobby, I nearly collided with two cops in uniform talking to Peter Piatek. Peter had a camera slung around his neck.

The cops turned. It was Anthony Ferrante. Next to him stood Chief Tedesco.

She frowned when she saw me. Then a smile twisted the edge of her mouth. "Perfect timing, Miss Smyth."

She stepped toward me. A loud click made me jump as something snapped onto my wrist. I looked down to see a handcuff.

"What's going on?" I asked, shuffling back a step.

"Bernie Smyth, I'm arresting you for the murders of Mark Lewis and Liz Lewis. Anything you say can—"

"Liz Lewis?"

I looked at Anthony.

His face was ashen. "We found her in her trailer," he said. "Stabbed in the back with a carving knife."

The floor tilted. My head spun. With my free hand, I grabbed Nat's arm to keep from falling.

"No," I muttered.

"Yes," Chief Tedesco said, triumphantly. "And your fingerprints are all over the knife."

A heavy silence hung over the hospital lobby. A click-click-click broke it as Peter Piatek, camera held up, snapped photos of me.

17

I groaned and thought, *Now who's going to make all those cannolis?*

Even as I faced a lifetime in prison for crimes I did not commit, all I could think was that I would miss the cannoli competition. Angelica would be stuck making 300 cannolis by herself. I preferred worrying about Angelica, because my own situation was so much worse.

The chair in the interrogation room dug into my legs and back. It was even more uncomfortable this time, because I couldn't move much—they'd cuffed my hands to the metal table.

Anthony sat across from me, and behind him was a wide mirror, beyond which another officer—or even the chief of police herself—might stand, listening to our conversation.

I sighed. Again. I'd been sighing a lot these past several hours. "Look, Anthony, you saw me at Liz's trailer."

"For the record," Anthony said, his eyes flicking to the side, as if he was just as aware of being watched as I was. "I saw you at the boathouse, Miss Smyth. Not at the scene of the crime."

Apparently we'd gone from first names back to formal address. He winced every time he called me Miss Smyth, though, which at least suggested he didn't like it much.

I tried to reason with Anthony. "Would I have killed Liz and then come out and chatted calmly? You know I didn't do this."

A manila file lay open with several sheets of paper and a pen, and Anthony shuffled the papers while he avoided making eye contact.

"Your prints match those on the murder weapon, Miss Smyth. Uh, the probable murder weapon. You were the last to see Liz Lewis alive."

"And did I attack Susan, too?"

"Susan Davis is not 100 percent sure it was a man who attacked her."

We had already been over this a dozen times. Anthony had revealed that after a couple hours of pacing up and down the path near the trailer, the police officers responsible for guarding Liz had become suspicious—they'd seen no movement from within. So they knocked on the door. When there was no answer, they'd gone inside and found Liz. She was dead. Stabbed in the back.

"How come I didn't have any blood on me when I left Liz's trailer?" I asked.

Anthony rubbed his chin. "You must have cleaned yourself off when you cleaned the murder weapon."

"When I cleaned the what?"

Anthony colored. "The knife." And then mumbled, "I shouldn't have said that."

"So the knife didn't have any blood on it?"

He gave his head a tiny shake.

The probable murder weapon, Anthony had said, as if it wasn't 100 percent certain. I recalled my visit to Liz and what

I'd seen there: the spartan interior, the books, the bed. And yes, there had been a knife in Liz's trailer.

A jolt went through me. Of course. I had touched that knife.

"This murder weapon," I said. "Was it by a knife block? Because after Liz threatened me with a knife, thinking I was an intruder, she handed it to me. That would explain my prints."

Anthony looked at me. The cogs in his mind were apparently turning. Finally, he said, "Yes, it would."

We started our volley of dialogue over again: me claiming I was innocent, he insisting the evidence pointed to my guilt. But I could see how skeptical he was, and finally, I called him out on it.

I leaned forward—as far as I could go with my hands cuffed—and I whispered, "Anthony, tell me honestly, do you even believe I'm guilty?"

"I can't answer that question. It's for a judge and jury to decide."

"Your boss, Chief Tedesco, has already decided."

"Chief Tedesco's a good cop," Anthony said quickly, defending her.

"But you don't always agree with her."

Silence.

"Lately," he mumbled, glancing over his shoulder at the mirror, "maybe less than usual."

Then he frowned. He straightened up in his chair. "Wait a minute, Miss Smyth. I'll be the one asking the questions, thank you very much."

He tried to sound authoritative, but I had rattled him.

I smiled. I could have kissed his face. Because he'd just admitted that he disagreed with Chief Tedesco. He was taking my side against hers. Maybe that meant I still had a sliver of hope.

"I touched that knife, and that's why it has my prints," I said. "But if I were a killer, and I took the time to clean the blood off the knife, why wouldn't I clean off the fingerprints?" Before Anthony could answer that, I plowed ahead. "No, it doesn't make sense, and you know it. If my prints are still on the handle of that carving knife, and you found no other knife, then that means the murder weapon is still out there."

Anthony frowned, obviously thinking it through.

"Maybe he needed the knife for another task," I said.

"Because when he attacked Susan, he failed. So he knew he'd have to return to finish the job."

"Right." I leaned forward in my chair, as much as I could with the handcuffs on. "Which means the murderer may still have the weapon with him."

"And if we find him with the knife, we'll have plenty of evidence to convict," Anthony said, getting excited.

"Plenty," I agreed.

Anthony closed the manila folder and got to his feet. But then turned, a frown on his face. "Bernie, unless we find a man with a ski mask and a bloody knife, you're still the prime suspect in two homicides. The killer would be supremely stupid—or desperate—to hold on to that kind of incriminating evidence. I don't see much hope."

∼

THE CONCRETE WALLS of the holding cell they placed me in put Liz's minimalism to shame. But at least there was a metal bench—firmly bolted to the floor—and I could catch some shut-eye while I waited for the next round of interrogation.

After drifting off to sleep, I woke up with a jerk.

I heard raised voices.

I looked around. The cell was dim, light from the corridor keeping the full dark of night at bay.

I stared at the dark ceiling and listened. One voice belonged to Anthony, the other to Chief Tedesco.

"The knife is clear evidence she didn't do it," Anthony said.

"The knife is nothing," Chief Tedesco snapped. "She's guilty."

"And you're—" Anthony cut himself off, as if he stopped himself from saying something he'd regret.

I was fully awake now and raised myself on one elbow, straining to hear.

Then Anthony spoke, after all. "You're obsessed, Diana. It's clear to me that your personal bias has clouded your vision. You're persecuting an innocent citizen, and I'm shocked that you can't see it yourself. Where's the chief of police I've always admired?"

What followed was a disturbing silence.

"And you're guilty of insubordination, maybe even obstruction of justice," she told him icily. "I should have your badge."

"Chief, I'd rather you take my badge than my integrity. I won't be an accessory to framing an innocent woman."

Someone stomped across the floor. A door slammed.

My heart was beating fast. I waited a long time for something else to happen—for voices to break the silence again—but all was quiet again.

I couldn't believe Anthony had stood up for me. He was a friendly, handsome guy, but I didn't think he was much of a detective. That might be true, but I had obviously underestimated his ethics.

I liked him twice as much. But if he lost his job, what good would that do me? He was my only friend in uniform. Without him, nothing stood between me and Chief Tedesco.

I lay back down and stared at the ceiling panels and fluorescent lights.

I remembered what Angelica had told me about how Chief Tedesco's husband and sister had betrayed her, leaving her alone. Despite everything, I felt a tug of sympathy for her. Maybe I was too tired to hate her for how she was treating me. Maybe I could relate to feeling alone…

I must have fallen asleep, because I heard the jangle of keys in a dream, and then the door to my cell swung open.

I sat bolt upright with a startled, "What?"

I blinked. Chief Tedesco stood in the doorway, a sour frown on her face.

"Here's what, Miss Smyth," she said, her voice raspy. "You're free to go."

I stared at her. "Come again?"

"We will no longer detain you on suspicion of murder."

She stood aside and motioned for me to come out. I got to my feet and stretched my back—my spine cracking and popping—and then sidled through the door, trying to ignore Tedesco's hard gaze.

Anthony stood a few paces away, arms crossed on his chest, a self-satisfied smile on his face.

"You did this?" I said.

"We did this," he said. "After I left you, I thought about what you'd said, and it became more and more obvious that the killer wouldn't hold on to that knife. It was too risky. So if he didn't leave it at the scene of the crime, where did it go?"

"You went back to the woods."

"I did," he said. "He probably tossed the weapon in the lake, I thought. But what if he didn't? What if he dumped it in the woods near the other attack?"

"By the Overlook."

"That's right. And that's where I found it. Close to where we found Susan. Although he'd wiped the handle clean of prints, Susan has identified the weapon as the one the attacker used."

I threw my arms around him and squeezed him.

He let out a little, "Oh," and then peeled me off, his face flushed with embarrassment.

"Just doing my job."

∼

As I walked out of the police station, the sun was rising over Carmine. Ahead of me lay the parking lot, and never had I seen such a beautiful sight. The low sun glinted off the backs of police cruisers. A bird fluttered from a tree down to an overflowing garbage can. Even the trash—candy-bar wrappers and crushed soda cans—looked beautiful.

My body ached, my head felt as heavy as lead and as fuzzy as a cotton ball—the awful effects of sleep deprivation—but my feet felt light and springy. I nearly tap danced down the steps. Losing my freedom sure made me appreciate it.

A truck pulled up to the curb, screeching to a halt, and I jumped back.

The side of the truck said, www.usps.com. The driver's window of the mail truck rolled down.

"Get in," Roberta LaRosa said.

Once I was comfortable in the passenger's seat, Roberta

eased the truck away from the curb. We rumbled slowly down the street.

Now and then a car drifted past us, but most of the town was still asleep. It was Saturday. The day of the big street festival. Soon, volunteers would make the final preparations, while the rest of town got ready for a day of fun and games—and tons of sugary goodies.

We took a long, meandering drive around the town's residential streets. She asked me about the murders, and I told her everything. It turned out she already knew most of it. She'd been keeping tabs on me, talking regularly with Chief Tedesco.

"You've got bad luck, Bernie," Roberta said. "Either that or you have a talent for getting into trouble."

It was probably both. But I didn't say that. I kept quiet. Eventually, Roberta would tell me why she'd sought me out, and I had a feeling it wouldn't be good.

"I should have seen the danger in placing you under Chief Tedesco's protection, since she, by her own admission, had been going through some personal stuff." She winced. Maybe because she'd heard about Tedesco's nightmarish ordeal with her sister and husband. "You've dodged a bullet and I doubt the chief of police will try to pin the crime on you again, but the whole thing has exposed you. I'm worried what this might mean for your safety."

"The dust will settle," I said. "I'll be fine. Carmine is safe."

Roberta shook her head. "I wish it were true. Have you read the news?"

I hadn't even checked my phone since getting it back from the police. I dug the phone out of my pocket and woke it from sleep.

Notifications clogged my lock screen, including several with "breaking news."

I opened Peter's news site and my heart nearly stopped. A single image dominated *The Carmine Enquirer*'s front page. A photo of me in handcuffs. The headline said, "A double-shot of murder? Barista arrested for stabbings."

I groaned. "This is bad."

"This is very bad," Roberta agreed. "In fact, given the attention this puts on you, I can't leave you here. The risk that Harry Casanova will discover you are hiding in Carmine is high. You have no choice. You have to leave."

My chest tightened. I couldn't breathe.

"Leave?"

Outside, we passed manicured lawns and modest ranch-style houses. One house had a lamppost carved to look like Frank Sinatra. On the front lawn of another, a sign said, "All Are Welcome." At that moment, it felt as though the sign spoke directly to me.

"I can't leave," I said, and realized with a jolt how true it was. "Since working at Moroni's, since making friends with Angelica and Nat, I've come to love Carmine. I can't go."

"If it's about the cabin in Alaska..."

"It's not about the cabin, Roberta. I can't move to Alaska or anywhere else. Carmine's the place for me. I can feel it in my bones."

I stared at her, feeling my words were inadequate and yet hoping and praying she'd understand.

She stared ahead at the road. "I'm sorry, Bernie. My number one priority is to keep you alive. Carmine is no longer safe."

"But—"

"That's all there is to say." She stopped the truck, the

engine still idling. We'd arrived at my house. "You have 24 hours to pack up and say your goodbyes."

I looked across the driveway at the quiet little ranch-style house. From the outside, the house looked asleep. In a day, it would be abandoned, and I would be on a plane heading for Anchorage and then to the far north.

I dug down deep into my brain, thinking of all the ways I could undo what had been done.

Solve the murder case. But that wouldn't stop Harry Casanova.

Convince Peter to pull the story. But I'd have to tell him the truth, and that would be too big a scoop for him to ignore.

After that, my brain came up empty. Too tired. All it could muster was a vague longing for warmth and sweetness.

I stared out the window.

Guess that was enough of a clue.

"Will you take me into town, please?"

"How you spend your last 24 hours in Carmine is your business." Roberta put the truck in drive. "Where to?"

"Moroni's," I said. "I have work to do."

18

Despite the early hour, people were already milling about on Garibaldi Avenue. None of the stalls had opened yet, but many locals were either helping with the setup or simply gawking.

A man was testing the giant popcorn machine. Two women were polishing the display case for fresh pasta. One stand overflowed with hand-carved and painted figures representing famous Italian-Americans: Dean Martin, Jon Bon Jovi, Mira Sorvino, and dozens more.

As I neared Moroni's, I bumped into Peter Piatek.

He shoved his phone at me, the audio recording app open and ticking away. "Miss Bernie Smyth, any comment on being released from police custody?"

"Cut it out, Peter. I've got nothing to say to you."

He stopped the recording.

"Off the record?"

"You have no idea how damaging your article about me was."

"The citizens of Carmine have a right to the latest news."

"Does the rest of the world as well?"

"Thanks to you, I've attracted hundreds of new readers to the site. This one story has had more views than anything since last year's pumpkin festival resulted in the second-largest pumpkin in New Jersey."

An icy hand ran down my spin. "Exactly how many people out of state have seen this?"

"Oh, quite a lot," he said. "There are people on both coasts, in the south, Midwest, you name it. Even a couple of views from Alaska."

Maybe I ought to tell Roberta that—it might convince her Alaska was no safer than New Jersey.

Peter patted my shoulder and smiled. "Get used to it, Bernie. You're famous."

I dragged my feet to the bakery, feeling unbearably heavy. Even if I somehow miraculously solved the case, my face was all over the internet. Harry Casanova was looking for me. How long before he found my photo on *The Carmine Enquirer* website?

I staggered into Moroni's. A wave of heavenly smells rolled over me—freshly ground coffee and baked sugar—and I drew in a deep breath of air. It steadied me a little. Then Angelica threw herself at me, wrapping me in a fierce embrace, and nearly knocking me off my feet.

"*Poverina*," she exclaimed.

We held each other for a while. Angelica's hair smelled of fried dough. It was possibly the most comforting smell in the world.

"You're wearing yesterday's clothes," she said. "Go home, shower, change. Do you need to get some sleep?"

I shook my head. "I'd rather be here making cannolis with you."

Angelica smiled ruefully. "Well, I do need a lot more cannolis."

I gave her a long look. "How bad is it?"

"Oh, there's nothing bad about the cannolis I've made so far. But I only have sixty so far. And that leaves—"

"Two hundred and forty."

"That's right," she said with a sigh. "And the fair opens in an hour."

I joined her in the kitchen, and we got to work. We made more cannoli shells. We made more ricotta cream. But even as we worked, my hands felt sluggish and my mind drifted off to unanswered questions.

Where was Mark's cousin, Steve?

What would he do about Susan still being alive?

And how had he ever thought he would get away with these murders?

If only there was a way to know where he was hiding.

At one point, Angelica glanced over at me. "You still thinking about the murders?"

I nodded.

She tsk-tsked. "Imagine how different everything would have turned out if Mark had taken Joanna's advice and made a will. Even if he'd refused to go to a lawyer or a notary, he could have made a handwritten one and that would have been legal, or so Joanna tells me. Just imagine. There would have been no point in killing him or anyone else."

I stared at Angelica.

"Are you all right, sweetie?"

"Angelica, you're a genius," I said and put down my spatula.

"I am?"

19

I called Nat, and when I'd finished telling him about my idea, he remained silent for a while.

Sitting on the couch in Angelica's office, I pressed the phone to my ear.

"But someone will recognize the handwriting," he finally said.

"Who?" I asked. "No one was really that close with Mark, and how often do you see someone's handwriting anyway? Besides, we won't need Steve to get so close that he can study the style. We just need to draw him out."

"All right, but what about Peter—you think he'll buy it?"

"Peter wants a story like this so badly, he won't question it. 'We've found a handwritten note hidden in one of Mark's possessions; if it turns out to be a will, it will significantly affect the murder investigation.' That's all we say. Peter will eat it up."

"And the cops?"

"Well…" I hesitated.

I glanced toward the doorway and cupped a hand over

my phone, hoping to mute the sound. It would be best if Angelica, at work in the bakery, didn't overhear me say this.

"I'll fill them in..."

"...when the time is right?" Nat said, finishing my sentence.

He understood me perfectly. The police would never agree to a plan like mine, and yet Chief Tedesco had sidetracked the investigation so badly, I feared Steve would find a clever way to escape.

We went back over our plans. We would contact Peter with the story, providing him with more of his beloved breaking news, plus a photo of a handwritten note on a legal pad, suitably blurry. Our story was going to be that we'd found the sheet of paper in Mark's kayak in the boathouse.

That was Nat's idea.

"Only place Mark seemed happy," he said. "So it stands to reason he'd keep something so precious hidden in his kayak."

"Right, and like Liz with her canoe, he'd keep his kayak, even after giving up all his other possessions."

"I bet there's probably an appendix to *A Moron's Step-by-Step Guide to Living with Less* that lists all the acceptable things to hold on to. You know, like a remote-controlled popcorn maker or a diamond-studded chess set. Essential stuff."

After planting the story, we'd wait for the news to spread. Eventually, if the plan worked, the killer would contact us.

"Except there won't be an 'us,'" Nat said.

"What do you mean?"

"I mean, you're too deeply involved in all this already. If your name is associated with finding the alleged will, Steve will get suspicious. But he doesn't know me. Plus, I work for the historical society—we're always digging up lost documents."

"Yeah, but..."

"I'll call Peter," Nat said emphatically. "He'll quote me, and it will be clear I found the will."

I didn't like the idea. "This could get dangerous, Nat."

"Which is why I will stay at the Old Mill with Jerry and whoever else is taking a break from the street fair. Steve won't make a move in a public place."

"Assuming there are people at the Old Mill."

"Not everyone loves a street fair," Nat said. "There'll be plenty of people. And Jerry. The guy's so talkative, he's like a one-man crowd."

He sounded confident. I felt less sure of the revised plan.

But the more I thought about it, the more I had to admit that he was right about me being too exposed. I'd chased Steve down the street—he knew I was on to him.

We agreed that as soon as Nat sent me a message from the Old Mill, I would head his way, while also alerting the cops.

"All right," I agreed. "The plan's in place."

"And afoot," Nat added.

After hanging up, I joined Angelica in the bakery and focused my attention on making the 300 cannolis Moroni's needed for the street festival. But as I piped ricotta cream into cannoli shells, it was difficult to ignore the hammering of my heart. Our attempt to draw out the killer probably wouldn't work. Step one would fail. Peter wouldn't believe the story and the plan would die. Part of me—a large part—would be relieved.

My hands got damp with sweat, and I had to stop and wipe them on my apron.

I got back to work.

Then jumped when my phone pinged and vibrated.

Quickly, I brushed the dough and flour off my hands and got the phone out of my pocket, fumbling and nearly dropping it.

My heart sprang into my throat. The notification on my screen said,

> "BREAKING NEWS: Murder victim's last will and testament found?"

∽

AFTER THE NEWS STORY BROKE, the waiting became nearly unbearable. I paced back and forth, and knocked over a bowl with ricotta cream. As I bent to pick it up, I rammed the back of my head into the tabletop above.

"Ouch!"

Angelica raised an eyebrow. She suggested I take a break from baking and instead take care of any customers that might come in.

Outside, the street fair was well under way, and the sound of music and talking and laughter roared into the bakery every time the door opened. In contrast, the soft jingle of the bell was barely audible.

Still, customers came off the street, and I sold many bags of pignoli and rainbow cookies, despite the same wares being available from the stand in the street. A woman in a baseball cap asked for cannolis. But below the "cannoli" label, the counter was bare—we had delivered them all to the stand outside.

"But they're sold out at the stand," the woman said, hands on her hips. "This is a disaster."

Just then Angelica emerged from the back with a tray of cannolis.

"Disaster averted," she told the woman. Then turned to me. "Here, Bernie, bring this tray to the stand. I've got another in the back I'll use for the shop."

I grabbed the tray and hurried into the street.

We shared the stall featuring Italian baked goods with Carlo's, and Maria took care of selling the wares. She thanked me when I handed her the tray of cannolis.

"They're selling like hot cakes," she said. Then added, "Really, the expression ought to be, 'They're selling like cannolis.'"

As I was unloading the tray, carefully placing the cannolis in the stand's glass case, I overheard a father and his toddler at a nearby stand with a display of colorful teddy bears, and it made me pause.

"No, Jimmy. You can't have the bear." The father's face was flushed. "I don't care how much you cry or scream, you ain't never gettin' that bear, all right? Never."

Tempted as I was to judge the father for his sharp tone, I reminded myself that I didn't have a toddler. What did I know? Maybe if my kid had the gimmes, I'd say the same thing. Or worse.

Regardless, it had awoken a memory. It wasn't so much the dad's words as his tone of voice. It had given me a sense of déjà vu. Where had I heard that before?

Of course. It reminded me of Carlo's account of Mark telling off Steve: "The cafe will never be yours."

The cafe property was at the heart of these murders. Dan had been tight-lipped about the sale he'd been working on with Mark, but maybe now that Liz had been killed and Susan attacked, he'd be more willing to reveal something about this secret real estate deal.

I was getting too antsy to wait behind the counter at the bakery, anyway. I had to do something. A detour to look for Dan would only take five minutes—I'd be back at Moroni's in no time.

Down the street at Russo's Realty, the front door was locked. A note in the window said, "Out on business. Please call and leave a message."

I spun around, intending to return to the bakery, and instead stopped, a glint of yellow having caught my eye.

I froze.

Across the street, Cafe Roma's steel shutters were down, the crime scene tape gone. Leaning against the steel shutters was a bicycle. It was canary yellow.

∾

TWO PEOPLE STOOD by the bicycle talking.

It was Peter Piatek and Emma Francis.

"Ah, the free bird," Peter said when he saw me coming toward them. "Any comment on your recent release?"

I ignored him. "Whose bicycle is this?"

Emma dropped her eyes, staring intently at her sneakers.

"It's mine," she mumbled.

Peter gave a sidelong glance at Emma, a questioning quirk forming at his brow. For a moment, I thought he would interrogate her, but even Peter seemed to have his limits.

"It was you who tried to run me down," I said.

She pressed her lips together, apparently refusing to speak. But her lips quavered, and then she broke down.

"Oh, I'm such an idiot. Such an idiot." She gazed at me, eyes glassy with the threat of tears. "I thought you were after

Nat, and I wanted to give you a warning, that was all. I swear to God I didn't want to hurt you. Just scare you. I don't know what I was thinking. Can you forgive me?"

She stared at me with doe-like earnestness—and although my body crackled with angry energy, there was little I could do to resist that kind of appeal. I clenched and unclenched my hands.

"Oh, what the heck," I said and exhaled. "You're forgiven."

I turned to Peter, who looked far too interested in our exchange. I jabbed a finger in his face. "And don't even think about turning this into a news story, Peter."

He waved away the idea. "No need. The reckless bicyclist story can die a quiet death."

Emma winced, no doubt at the title he'd conferred on her, but he continued, unfazed.

"I've got plenty of big stories these days. Did you hear about my big scoop?"

He told me all about how a handwritten will had been discovered, presumably belonging to Mark.

"Already the online story's got as many views as my last one, and the other blog posts about the murder case are trending. Lots of readers are interested in what happens in Carmine. Seriously, Bernie, you should thank me."

I couldn't follow his logic. "I'd thank you if my name wasn't all over the internet."

"But see, that's the beauty of the internet," he said, sounding earnest. "It connects people. It even *reconnects* people. And here's a great example of it: After posting the story about you, an old high school friend of yours contacted me. He wants to reconnect with you and asked me if you really live in Carmine, which obviously you do."

I grabbed Peter's arm. I must have squeezed hard, because he winced and tried to pull away.

"What old high school friend?"

"Jeez, Bernie, relax. Just some guy."

"What guy?"

"Some guy named Harry."

20

Turning away from Emma and Peter, and moving in a daze, I wove through the crowd. Happy, smiling faces flitted past me, but I took no notice of them. My mind was filled with Harry's face—hair disheveled, teeth bared, eyes bulging with bloodlust.

Harry Casanova knew where I was. He was coming.

Even if I could solve Mark and Liz's murders before U.S. Marshall Roberta LaRosa rode into Carmine in her mail truck to ship me off to Alaska, would it matter? The cat was out of the bag and now Harry was going to strangle it. I shuddered at the image of myself as a poor cat.

Should I call Roberta? For what—so she could whisk me away to Alaska? As long as there was a shred of hope that I could stay in this town, I'd hold on to it.

Should I contact the police instead? Chief Tedesco might not react well. Would she ignore my plea for help or lock me up again?

No, I would continue with the plan to draw out the killer. I could only hope that Harry took a while to get to New Jersey.

Meanwhile, I'd have to keep my eyes open.

As I paid more attention to my surroundings, I noticed a couple of people studying me. One guy nudged his girlfriend, nearly knocking a cup of coffee out of her hand.

"Hey," she complained. "What?"

"It's her," the guy whispered. "From the news."

Oh, great. Of course I should have expected this. If Harry Casanova knew that I'd been a suspect in the murder case, so would half of Carmine, not to mention the surrounding county.

My heart sank. What were the odds that I would solve this case, clear my name, and slip back into obscurity? One in a million.

I checked my phone. No messages from Nat. I texted him, just in case, expecting an immediate response. But nothing came.

Probably busy talking to Jerry.

Well, drifting around the street festival would solve nothing. I'd better find Dan Russo. Maybe Angelica knew where he was.

Ahead of me, I saw a couple of uniforms. As if my day wasn't already hard enough, I once again had to face Chief Tedesco. I wished I could turn and walk away, but she'd already seen me.

She surprised me by doing what I'd considered doing: fleeing.

She gave me a wide-eyed, deer-in-headlights look, and abruptly turned and stalked off.

Anthony, who'd been walking by her side a moment ago, approached me, shaking his head. Together, we gazed off at the chief as she shouldered her way through the crowd.

"What was that about?" I asked.

"She's embarrassed," Anthony said. "Ashamed, actually.

After all, she arrested the wrong person, and all because of sloppy police work. She compromised the investigation. That's about the worst thing a cop can do, according to her own rulebook."

As we walked down the sidewalk, side by side, he described Chief Diana Tedesco as meticulous and conscientious, a person who lived and breathed the idea of protecting and serving.

"But since her divorce, she's been off-kilter. Not sleeping. Skipping meals. Behaving erratically."

"I heard she separated from her husband," I said, remembering my promise to Angelica not to spread gossip.

"Yeah, she took it pretty hard," Anthony said lightly, and I wondered how much sympathy and understanding Chief Tedesco had gotten.

Maybe she'd faced indifference or even nastiness from people around her, and she'd kept to herself, trying to hide her troubles. That sounded familiar. I knew a thing or two about hiding away. Though I couldn't imagine the pain Chief Tedesco must have felt when her sister and her husband betrayed her. After such an awful discovery, it would be easy to lose your way.

Chief Tedesco had equated my "betrayal" of Jay Casanova with that of her husband and sister. I had become a stand-in, a scapegoat. It wasn't right, and it wasn't fair, but at least her erratic behavior made sense to me.

"She reacted strongly to you," Anthony said.

"Yeah, I seem to have a powerful effect on some people."

I was thinking of Jay and Harry Casanova, but Anthony, it appeared, was thinking of something else.

"Yes, you do have a powerful effect," he said, an odd emphasis on the last two words.

He cleared his throat and stared at me with determination, as if he wanted to tell me something important. *Oh, no. Not now.* If this had been an old movie, the soundtrack would have introduced a slow, romantic violin.

"Bernie..." he said.

He stopped, forcing me to stop as well.

"Bernie," he repeated. "Listen, I..."

Behind him was Carlo's restaurant. Unable to decide where to look—his intense stare was like a bright light and I got a sudden case of stage fright—I stared through the window.

All the air left my lungs, and I gasped.

"Bernie—you all right?"

Inside Carlo's, at a table by the window, sat Dan Russo and Joanna Parisi, and they were having coffee with an out-of-towner.

It was Mark's cousin, Steve. The killer.

21

"What's wrong?" Anthony said, as I pushed past him. "What did I say?"

I shouldered my way through a gaggle of teenage girls and flung open the door to Carlo's.

Carlo stood at the table closest to the door, having just delivered a cup of coffee to a woman in a New Jersey Devils cap, and he turned, smiling.

"Bernie," he said, bringing his hands together in a clasp and shaking them. "What a relief it was when I heard they released you. Are you hungry? Everyone's hungry after a night in the lockup, right? Because of the street festival, we're open all day for food, coffee, whatever people want."

I rushed up to him and grabbed him by the arm.

"Carlo, this is important. Is that the mystery man you saw with Mark?"

Carlo nodded. "Imagine my surprise when I saw him come through the door." He scratched his goatee. "All this time, apparently, Dan and Joanna knew him. You see, his name is Steve, and he's—"

I didn't wait to hear what Carlo was going to say. I strode

across the room, eager to get to Steve, before he slipped away again.

The three sat at a table by the window. To escape through the front door, Steve would have to get past me.

As I approached, all three of them—Dan, Joanna, and Steve—looked up, surprised.

Steve frowned.

"You're Steve," I said.

"And you're the woman who chased me down the street."

"This time you're not getting away."

Steve's mouth twisted into a grimace. "Dan, Joanna, can we please find a place where I won't be bothered?"

He half rose in his seat.

"Sit down," I ordered, grabbing his shoulder and pushing him back into his seat.

Forget about softie Bernie Smyth; tough-as-nails Eve Silver wouldn't let this guy run.

"I'll have Carlo's crawling with cops in the blink of an eye. Then you can tell them all about how you murdered your cousin."

Steve let out a bark of laughter. "My cousin? Murder? What are you talking about?"

Again, he gave Dan a look and then Joanna, widening his eyes, as if asking for their help with this madwoman.

"Easy now, Bernie," Dan said. "There's been a misunderstanding."

"You can say that again. The cops have pointed to me as the killer, but the guy's sitting right here in Carlo's drinking coffee."

"No, Bernie. This is Steve Tufte, a business developer. He's been interested in buying property in town. In fact, he was ready to buy Cafe Roma, but Mark's untimely death put a stop to that deal." He addressed Steve again. "Steve, this is Bernie Smyth. She works at Moroni's Italian Bakery next door, but she used to work for Mark Lewis." He cleared his throat, as if embarrassed. "Apparently, she's got a little mixed up."

Steve leaned back in his chair and then ran a hand across his brow. "You think I killed Mark?"

"Right," I said, trying to sound confident. But something about all this wasn't right. In fact, it was very wrong.

"So you didn't chase me because of my burger franchise?"

"Burger franchise?"

"Hungry Eye Burgers. I was planning to buy Cafe Roma, tear it down, and build a burger franchise. The press and angry community groups have already hounded me in other towns—they've dubbed my restaurants 'stinky eyesores'—and I thought you were one of them, trying to scare me away from investing in Carmine."

I had a vague recollection of a story about the burger franchise on *The Carmine Enquirer* news site. Still, how did Steve's burger franchise relate to his family connections? Had Mark promised him a good deal for the cafe?

"Did being Mark's cousin play a role in all this?"

"Mark's cousin?" Steve shook his head. "I met Mark a few times because of the sale of the property—more times than I'd thought necessary, because he got upset at the price I offered."

"He walked out on you at Carlo's because you disagreed on the price?"

"That's right. But prior to the property negotiations, I'd never met him before. I'd never even been to Carmine before. I live in Montclair."

Dan and Joanna both nodded, corroborating what Steve

had said. At that moment, Maria approached the table with a plate of cannolis, courtesy of Moroni's.

"Maria," I said. "You told me Steve was Mark's cousin."

Maria shrugged. "To be honest, I'd only seen him around a couple of times, and I only learned later that he was Mark's cousin. Susan told me, and she ought to know, right?"

"That's odd," Joanna said. "You're right: Susan, of all people, ought to know who Mark's relatives are. We looked at the family tree together. I've even explained all the legal stuff to her. In fact, with poor Liz dead, there's only one surviving next of kin."

"Susan," I said, my throat constricting. The words came out in a whisper. "It's always been Susan."

22

Nat didn't answer his phone. I called and called, each time reaching voicemail.

Outside on Garibaldi Avenue, I spun around myself, frantically looking for a way to get to the Old Mill. It was a long walk. Even if I ran, I was sure I'd get there too late. Could I hitch a ride? Get a taxi? But the time that would take...

Across the street stood Emma and Peter, still talking, Emma's canary yellow bike leaning against Cafe Roma's shutters.

I rushed over, and Emma took a step backward, holding up her hands defensively. She probably still expected me to reciprocate her attack.

"I need to borrow this," I told her.

"Sure," she said, her brow furrowed with worry. "Of course."

She unlocked the bike and handed it to me, giving me another wary look. Did she really think I planned to ride around on her bicycle and, when she least expected it, try to run her down? That's what her nervous gaze suggested. If so, her mind worked in strange ways.

But I didn't have time to worry about Emma Francis.

People clogged the sidewalk and the street. I pulled the bicycle down the middle of Garibaldi, dodging people eating zeppoles and waving Italian flags.

Finally, I got to the traffic barriers. I swung up on the bike and pushed the pedals into action. The wheels spun on the blacktop. I lowered my head over the handlebars and sped up the street.

My mind ran over what I'd learned. All this time, I'd operated on the assumption that Steve was Mark's cousin, but it had been a lie, planted by Susan to distract attention from her efforts. Maria's confident claim that it was Mark's cousin convinced me, and why would anyone question such a basic fact?

I shook my head. Eve Silver might have, but amateur sleuth Bernie had failed to catch the lie.

I pedaled faster and faster. A car pulled out of a parking spot and I swerved into the middle of the street, barely dodging an oncoming car. The driver honked his horn and yelled out of his window, "*Stunad!*"

I steadied the bike again, and pedaled hard.

Susan had caused another distraction—a more serious one: the attack in the woods. Of course, the man in the ski mask was an invention. Susan had wanted to kill Liz, and time was running out. Finding Liz during the day had proved difficult, and Susan couldn't do it at night. At the Old Mill, she had told me so herself—her stepfather kept her on a strict nighttime curfew. Hence her little "lunch break" at the Overlook.

She'd planted the idea of Steve as the killer in my mind, but it backfired: I went snooping around the trailer, complicating her plans. I even called the cops. So she needed to draw us all away.

She called the police, pretending someone had attacked her. Then turned off her phone. That drew Anthony away from the boathouse. The drive to the Overlook would take him all the way around the lake, leaving plenty of time. Once Nat and I had left too, Susan could freely visit Liz. The murder done, she ran back through the woods, and slashed her arms to make her story about an attacker believable. Her run from Liz's trailer back to the Overlook took time, which was why the cops couldn't find her at first.

My heart raced as I turned onto Lake Road, leading up the hill to the Old Mill. I pedaled furiously. The wind rushed past my ears, but it felt like cycling through sand—it would never be fast enough.

Why didn't you ask Dan or Joanna for a ride? Or find Anthony?

But getting to a car might have taken just as much time.

The hill rose into the woods, steeper than I remembered.

Because you were in a car or walking. Biking—and biking fast—is a heck of a lot harder.

I pushed down on the pedals, my thigh muscles burning with the effort. My chest hurt from breathing hard. I was no Giro d'Italia rider, but I wouldn't give up.

Nat was in danger. I knew it.

Susan had planned to kill Mark and Liz, but the murders had gone awry. In both cases, because I'd shown up—and so Susan had taken desperate action, including inventing the mystery cousin, a fiction the cops eventually would have discovered to be a lie.

Realizing that didn't comfort me. Susan was desperate. That meant she was dangerous.

I pedaled even harder. Up ahead, the old sawmill building came into view.

I swerved across the road and came to a skidding halt in the parking lot, gravel dancing around my tires. I threw down the bike and raced to the front door.

Inside, the jukebox was playing a Johnny Cash song and Jerry was standing behind the bar calmly wiping a pint glass with a cloth. He gave me a silent nod.

"Where's Nat?" I asked breathlessly, looking around and seeing no one else. The Old Mill was empty. Everyone was at the street festival. "Did he leave? Did he leave with someone?"

Jerry nodded. My heart sank.

"Susan."

I groaned. "Any idea where they went?"

"Boathouse."

Nat must have stalled by saying he'd left the document where he found it—in Mark's kayak at the boathouse. But I'd never get all the way to the lake on Emma's bike in time.

"Jerry, do you have a car? Can you take me to the boathouse? It's an emergency."

Jerry shrugged. "Sure."

He put down the glass and the kitchen towel.

I only hoped we'd get there in time. Mark's fake will would undo all of Susan's plans, which meant she'd want to destroy it and leave no witnesses.

Jerry came around the bar, and I turned to go with him to his car.

The door to the Old Mill clicked shut. A man stood in front of it. He slid the deadbolt, locking us in.

He spun around, and my heart seized up.

Harry Casanova flipped open a switchblade.

"Bernadette."

23

Harry took a step toward me with the switchblade held out. His wild, red-rimmed eyes suggested he'd been feeding off more than hatred. Cocaine, probably.

He took another step toward me and I moved back.

Jerry, who maybe had more experience with these things, took three steps back and a couple sideways, and within moments, he'd reached the end of the bar.

Harry had me to himself.

"I've dreamed of this moment," Harry said, licking his lips. "I've promised Jay to send pictures."

"How cute. You guys share photos?" I glanced around. No weapons in sight. Nothing I could grab or even hide behind. I tried to keep him distracted. "Must be fun to see behind-the-scenes footage of Jay's new career in corrections."

I honestly wasn't trying to rile him up. I was nervous. So I talked.

He growled and swiped the blade at me.

I backed away and something hard hit my back. I glanced over my shoulder. The bar.

I caught sight of Jerry. He had slipped around the counter and stood further down, where his row of clean pint glasses sat on a dish towel. He had his phone out and was tapping away at the screen.

A memory flashed across my mind. In Episode 8 of *Silver & Gold*'s second season ("Murder on the Rocks"), a hitman cornered Eve Silver in a cocktail bar. Eve used a bottle of priceless, aged brandy to parry her enemy's attacks with a knife. It gave me an idea—and I didn't need priceless, aged brandy.

"Jerry," I said. "A pint, please."

He seemed to understand, because he grabbed an empty glass and, with a professional flick of the wrist, sent it skating across the counter. It slid into my open hand. I grasped it, just as Harry dove forward to stab me in the stomach.

Clank!

His blade went into the pint glass.

His eyebrows shot up. The impact clearly jarred him. He'd no doubt expected soft flesh, instead he got metal on glass.

He fumbled with the knife, but before he could grasp it for another attack, I tossed the pint glass aside, bringing the switchblade along for the ride.

The glass rolled across the floorboards. The knife slid away.

Harry tugged at something in his jacket pocket—maybe another knife—but before he could do whatever he'd intended, I had kneed him in the groin and he doubled over with an audible "Oof!"

I didn't lose an instant. I rushed across the floor and snatched up the knife.

I swiveled around, brandishing the switchblade.

"Don't move," I said.

There was a loud, splintering crack, and the Old Mill's front door crashed open.

"Don't move," Chief Tedesco said, her gun drawn.

She eyed Harry by the bar, Jerry by his pint glasses, and me, standing in the middle of the floor with a switchblade.

"More knives, Miss Smyth?" she asked. "I thought you'd learned to steer clear of knives by now."

With a sinking heart, I realized how this might look. Apparently, Harry did too.

"This woman's crazy," he said. "She tried to attack me."

For a moment, we all stared at each other: I stared at Harry, he stared at Chief Tedesco, Chief Tedesco stared at me, and then I returned her gaze.

A satisfied smile spread across Chief Tedesco's face.

"Games up, Harry Casanova."

"I'm not—"

"I know who you are. *Maron'*, I ought to. I have an autographed photo of you and your brother on my wall."

"Careful," I said. "He's got something in his pocket."

Stupid me. By telling Chief Tedesco that, it gave Harry the split second distraction he needed.

He whipped out a gun. "Didn't want to draw attention to myself, but so be it. Plan B will be messy. I won't be sorry to see another pig hit the killing floor."

Harry was a failed screenwriter—and I could see why. Clearly, his dialogue was never his strong suit.

He aimed the gun at Chief Tedesco.

I didn't dare to look; I didn't dare to look away.

Chief Tedesco did nothing, simply staring with a kind of cold smugness at her enemy.

Harry pressed the trigger. Nothing happened.

"Safety catch, idiot," a voice said behind Harry.

He whipped around. Anthony stood behind the counter, gun aimed at Harry.

"Drop your weapon."

Harry, realizing that the game was up, finally saw some sense. He crouched down, placing the gun on the floor. He put up his hands.

"You'll regret this," he snarled as Anthony came around the counter and cuffed him and read him his rights.

"Everyone says that," Chief Tedesco said, holstering her gun. "Don't be such a cliché."

That seemed to hurt Harry more than the cuffs. He narrowed his eyes at her.

"You'll—" he spluttered. "I'll—"

But he'd run out of dialogue.

24

The tires on the police cruiser ripped up gravel as we tore out of the Old Mill's parking lot. Blood rushed in my ears as I clung to the sides of the passenger seat.

Chief Tedesco jerked the steering wheel to the left, and we swerved onto Lake Road. The lights overhead flashed, but she kept the sirens off.

"No need to warn Susan that we're coming," she said.

Anthony was taking Harry Casanova to the police station, while Chief Tedesco and I had teamed up to save Nat.

This day was full of surprises.

As the car flew over bumps in the road, Chief Tedesco filled me in on what had brought her to the Old Mill.

"Officer Ferrante and I were patrolling the street festival when I caught sight of a man I recognized. Harry Casanova. Obviously, seeing him set off alarm bells. There could only be one reason he'd come all the way from Los Angeles to Carmine."

"Me."

"That's right. So we followed him. He drifted around town asking about you, claiming to be an old high school buddy. For a while, we lost sight of him. Emma said you'd taken her bike, and then Primo Leone, the taxi driver, told us he'd taken a guy matching Harry's description to the Old Mill. As we were heading up Lake Road, we got a text message from Jerry about trouble at the bar. Anthony went in the back; I took the front. The rest, you know."

"You saved my life."

Tedesco gave a curt, acknowledging nod. "Now tell me about Susan."

As quickly as I could, I filled her in on how Susan murdered Mark and Liz, and then explained what Nat and I had planned—our effort to draw out the killer by planting a story about a will.

"That plan of yours," Tedesco said, eyeing me sternly, "was stupid."

I stared straight ahead, pressing my lips together. Anger ran through my arms like electricity. I was furious that Tedesco would call our plan stupid. She'd pushed me into this.

As if she knew my thoughts, she said, "Look, I didn't make things easy for you. Maybe I left you with nothing but stupid options."

"You're right, though," I said with a sigh. Nat was at the boathouse, his life in danger, and my anger felt more like fear. What if Susan killed him? "It was a stupid plan."

"Sometimes stupid works. It would've worked for Eve Silver. Besides, *you* figured out Susan did it, not the police. Not me."

For a while, neither of us spoke. The car jumped over a pothole and Tedesco steadied it.

Then said, quietly, "By the way, you were great on

Silver & Gold. Ever since I watched the show on TV, I wanted to be her, Eve Silver. I felt a special kinship with her—and I wondered what it would be like to kiss Adam Gold, the way she did. I mean, the way you did with Jay Casanova."

Another long silence. She bit her lip, staring straight ahead. This confession, no doubt something she hadn't shared with anyone else, visibly embarrassed her. Since her husband and her sister had left her, maybe she had no one left to talk to. Again, I felt a stab of sympathy for her.

"Like moldy cheese in an ashtray," I said, breaking the silence.

Tedesco raised an eyebrow.

"Kissing Jay Casanova. It was like licking moldy cheese from an ashtray. Not even the tasty French kind. He has horrible halitosis, probably from too much acidic food and alcohol and coffee. And he smokes a pack a day. His breath is downright rotten. I always dreaded the kissing scenes. Every one of them. It was hell."

There was another long silence.

Then Tedesco said, "Huh."

∼

"Stay here," Chief Tedesco said. "Backup will arrive soon."

She'd parked the car down the shoulder of the road a couple hundred yards from the boathouse, not wanting to roll into the gravel parking lot and alert Susan.

"I'm coming with you," I said.

"You're staying here," she insisted. "That's an order."

As I watched her run down the street, gun drawn, I dug my fingers into my thighs, mumbling to myself, "You've done enough, Bernie. Stay here."

Chief Tedesco had not just told me to stay. She'd given me an order, like she gave Anthony orders.

An order's an order, he might say. But then he was a cop. I wasn't.

I opened the car door and slipped out.

Mimicking Tedesco's crouch, I ran down the road, heading toward the boathouse. I moved along the grassy shoulder, with the road to my left and the trees to my right.

Through the trees, I caught glimpses of the lake. I slowed down as I came to the dirt drive that branched off from Lake Road and led to the boathouse.

Up ahead, Tedesco had climbed the steps to the boathouse, and she was inching her way toward the entrance, her back to the wooden wall, gun held high.

I held my breath as she rounded the corner, aiming her gun.

"Freeze," she called out, and then, "Nat, is that you?"

She stepped into the darkness, out of sight.

I cursed and ran, following in her path to where wooden steps led up from the parking lot to the wide boathouse entrance.

Beyond the boathouse, the lake was still. Birds chirped in the trees. Not a leaf rustled. The peacefulness, normally so appealing, made my skin crawl.

The feeling only grew stronger as I neared the entrance to the boathouse. I shivered. Again, I remembered that time in *Silver & Gold*—Episode 9 of Season 6 ("Drowning Man") —when Eve Silver faced the killer in a boathouse. Both the fictional boathouse and this very real one were painted red. Both had wide, gaping mouths leading into cool, damp darkness.

I pressed my back to the wooden wall the way Tedesco had. Unlike her, though, I had no gun. Pausing briefly at the edge of the entrance, I took a deep breath and peered around the corner.

Chief Tedesco stood in the middle of the boathouse. Bright light filled the opening to the dock beyond. Tedesco, a dark outline, moved toward the glare. Shadowy boats surrounded her—overturned on racks or hanging from ropes strung to the ceiling.

Near the entrance, a couple of yards from me, lay a stack of oars. Further along stood a pile of boxes. An old fishing net hung from a wall. Below, two fishing coolers gaped open, drying out.

As Tedesco took another step toward the sunbathed dock, I squinted to see better.

Out on the dock stood a lone figure.

My heart skipped a beat.

Nat stood as still as a statue. His hands were bound. His mouth covered with packing tape.

But where was Susan?

"Nat." Tedesco looked to the left and to the right, and then straight ahead again. "Where's Susan?"

Nat didn't move. Even from a distance, I could see the wide-eyed fear on his face. His bangs covered one eye, but the other darted back and forth. What did he want to say? What warning was he hoping to convey?

My heart pounded in my chest.

Susan's here. Somewhere.

Movement in the gloomy boathouse caught my eye. To the left of Tedesco, a shadow moved under a boat. It slid toward her. An object caught a ray of light, flashing as it emerged from the blackness.

A knife.

Tedesco whipped around, as if she'd heard a sound. She

turned to her right, aiming her gun at the shadows. But Susan pounced from the left.

The oars. I remembered how Eve Silver, before the script rewrite, had saved Adam Gold from the killer.

I rushed toward the stack of oars nearby and grabbed one. Raising it over my shoulder like a javelin, I flung it at Susan's legs.

Susan lunged at Chief Tedesco, bringing down the knife to bury it in her back, just as the oar caught her between the shins.

She let out a scream.

Tedesco spun around. And fired her gun.

The bullet struck the rack of kayaks, and the tower teetered. Then collapsed. The clatter was ear deafening.

When the falling kayaks had settled, I saw Chief Tedesco standing over Susan, gun aimed at her.

Susan's legs had gotten tangled in the oar and she lay on her back, unarmed.

She stared wide-eyed at Chief Tedesco. "My God, you almost shot me," she said, her amazement replaced with an indignant glare. "You could have injured me. Do you have any idea what that could have done to my acting career?"

~

I PULLED off the tape covering Nat's mouth.

"Ouch!" he said.

"Good thing you don't have a mustache," I said.

Once I got the rope off his wrists, I threw my arms around him and we hugged each other tight.

"I thought—"

"Yeah, I also thought—"

"But you're—?"

"I'm fine," Nat said. "A little rattled, that's all."

Sirens wailed in the distance. Looking across the lake, I saw flashes of police cruisers flitting through the trees, and a moment later, their tires churned up the gravel in the parking lot.

Nat and I joined Chief Tedesco in the boathouse.

"I thought I told you to stay in the car," she told me.

But she couldn't hide her smile. It was a bright smile, lighting up her face.

"I'm so glad you ignored me, Bernie."

Chief Tedesco and one of her officers led Susan off to a patrol car. By then, I realized I'd lost sight of Nat. He wasn't outside with the cops. He wasn't on the dock. Where had he gone?

"Nat?"

"Check this out."

I gazed into the shadows, blinking.

Nat was crouched down by the heap of kayaks that had fallen when Tedesco's bullet had hit the rack. He pushed aside the fallen kayaks, obviously searching for something.

"I stalled Susan by telling her Mark's will was hidden in the boathouse," Nat said. "She insisted on seeing it, of course, and I knew I'd run out of time. I pretended to search Mark's kayak. When I couldn't produce a will, she'd know it was all a ruse, and then get rid of me. Imagine my surprise, then, when I found this..."

He rummaged around in a kayak.

"When Susan saw it, she went nuts—thankfully, she heard a car approaching in the distance and got busy tying me up."

He threw a helmet over his shoulder. Then a life vest. Finally, he straightened up and held out an object.

It was an old, dog-eared paperback. Part of the front

cover was missing, but the title was still clear: *A Moron's Step-by-Step Guide to Living with Less.*

"Mark's book," I said, recognizing it. "So, this is where he put it."

"And this was his bookmark."

Nat removed the piece of paper I'd seen Mark use as his bookmark, a sheet from a yellow legal pad.

"This is no ordinary bookmark."

He handed it to me, and I unfolded it.

At the top, it said, "Last Will & Testament of Mark Lewis."

25

When we got back to town, a mob blocked the entrance to Moroni's. Half the visitors to the street festival must have crowded around the door. But the cafe-bakery was closed, and as I fought my way forward, a handwritten sign in the window came into view:

Sorry, no more cannoli.

"Oh, no," I said. "Angelica's cannoli competition."

My approach set off a chorus of complaints:

"Hey, lady, wait your turn."

"I was here first. Get back in line."

Ignoring the complaints, I rushed forward and unlocked the door and pulled it open.

The little bell jingled and Nat waved off the people who wanted to follow us inside, easing the door back into place and turning the lock.

Inside, Angelica sat at a table, her head down on the surface, her arms around it, hiding her face. Was she crying?

Had she lost the cannoli competition—and how much was it my fault for neglecting her during the past couple of days?

I felt a deep tug of guilt in my gut.

"Angelica?" I asked softly, sitting down next to her and putting a hand on her shoulder. "Are you all right?"

She started a little under my touch, and then slowly raised her head. Her eyes were bleary. She blinked.

"Oh," she said and yawned. "I fell asleep."

I studied her red eyes, her haggard look. "Have you been crying? I thought maybe..." I swallowed. "The cannoli competition."

Angelica lifted her head and reached above her head, stretching her arms.

"The competition?" she asked, sounding dazed from sleep. Then her eyes widened. "Oh, the competition."

My heart beat faster. Had she actually fallen asleep and missed it?

Then a big smile broke out on her face.

"*Mia cara,* see for yourself."

She gestured at something over my shoulder. I turned. On the wall, between a print of a gondola drifting down a Venetian canal and one of the Ponte Vecchio bridge in Florence, hung a framed certificate.

In gold letters, it said, "Moroni's Italian Bakery—#1 Cannoli in New Jersey."

I let out a shriek and threw my arms around Angelica, and we both laughed. Nat congratulated Angelica with a high five.

"This is amazing, Angelica," I said. "Tell me everything."

The judges of the competition had agreed unanimously: Moroni's cannolis with chopped pistachios were the best. The effect of the announcement, however, was to send the entire street full of people over to Moroni's to buy cannolis—a demand that far exceeded the supply.

"I planned on having 300 cannolis ready," Angelica said. "I would have needed twice as many. Within an hour, I'd sold them all, and by the time I sold everything else—pignoli, pizzelle, amaretti, you name it—I had to put a sign in the window to stop people from crowding in."

She motioned toward the glass display case—it was empty. Only crumbs remained.

"After that, I was so exhausted, I sat down and must have fallen asleep."

She put a hand to her chest, embarrassed. "But look at me gabbing away. Earlier on, I heard sirens. What have I missed?"

"It's a long story," I said.

"Good," she said. "I like long stories. Sit down. I'm making us all coffees."

When she'd made us all a caffe lungo each, she excused herself and went into the back. She returned with a plate. On the plate sat three cannolis.

"What's this?" I said. "You said they were all sold out."

"My grandmother always said, 'In every batch, save a bunch for the bakers, and the bakers' kin.' It's a good rule." She gave me a wink. "Because who doesn't need a cannoli at the end of a killer day like this?"

I couldn't argue with that.

We each bit into our cannoli. The shell crunched pleasantly in my mouth and mixed with the heavenly ricotta. I closed my eyes, enjoying the moment.

This was the good life.

THE NEXT MORNING, I woke to the sound of a vehicle outside. I peeked through the blinds in my bedroom and saw the mail truck idling in my driveway.

I pulled on a pair of jeans and a t-shirt and, in the hallway, my sneakers.

Outside my front door, the air was cool and fresh, the humid weather swept away by a north-easterly breeze. I drew in a deep breath, savoring the scent of grass and roses from nearby yards.

U.S. Marshall Roberta LaRosa was waiting for me behind the wheel.

"Ready?" she asked.

I scooted onto the passenger-side seat.

Roberta put the truck in reverse and soon we were rumbling pleasantly down the street.

As we rolled down the street, we passed a man in a green baseball cap who was tugging his dog leash, his Irish setter busy sniffing a tree. A woman bent down and picked up the newspaper from her driveway, and waved at the mail truck. Roberta turned into another neighborhood. On Pavarotti Street, we saw deer grazing on the dewy grass. The world was at peace.

Roberta gazed out the window. "You really like it in Carmine, huh?"

"The computer was right."

"The computer?"

"Yeah, the computer you told me chose the town based on 399 factors."

"Yes. The computer."

I glanced at her. She didn't look back. Roberta's reaction struck me as odd, but I couldn't figure out why.

I decided I was done with mysteries for now, though, and returned my attention to the scenic ride.

We drove along in silence, watching Carmine wake up to a new day. Another mail truck came rumbling toward us, and as it passed, the driver held up a hand in greeting.

"A colleague?" I asked, wondering if every mail truck was, in fact, a cover for a U.S. Marshall on business.

"I'm friendly with the local USPS team. Nice folks." She turned the truck down another street. Then said, "I still think you'd be safer in Alaska. But Harry's in detention, and he's confessed to attempting to kill you. Not just that, the guy blabbed about his involvement in the drugs and guns business—he'll join his brother in prison for a long, long time. Still, you never know what crazy Casanova-loving nuts are lurking out there."

"What does Chief Tedesco say?"

"Oh, you know what she says. She's got nothing but good things to say about you and your future in Carmine. If she weren't vouching for you, I wouldn't allow you to stay. I don't know how you won her over, but you've clearly made a friend for life."

She turned the steering wheel, and we drifted onto Garibaldi Avenue. She pulled up to the curb by Moroni's Italian Bakery. The curtains were still drawn.

Good. Angelica isn't up earlier than she needs to be.

"Wonder what will happen to the cafe," Roberta said.

Across the street, Cafe Roma looked abandoned. The metal shutters were down, the windows closed on the first floor.

"Mark Lewis bequeathed everything he owned to a charity for single mothers," I said. "I guess we'll see if they sell the property or use it for one of their thrift shops."

Roberta shook her head. "I can't believe you actually found his handwritten will. So Susan's crazy scheme to inherit had been pointless from the beginning."

"If she'd known about Mark's will, she might not have killed him or Liz. But then again, maybe she would have looked for the will, destroyed it, and then committed murder, anyway. She was crazy. All because she wanted money to launch her Hollywood acting career, and she couldn't wait. She couldn't wait to become famous."

Her motive, which had emerged after her arrest, reminded me of the reason Jay Casanova, despite already being rich and successful, had smuggled drugs and guns: He had wanted more, faster. It seemed Susan suffered from the same greedy impulse.

I no longer had to worry about Susan Davis anymore, though.

I gazed out at Garibaldi Avenue. Carlo's Restaurant. Parisi & Parisi's. Russo's Realty. Milano Books. Further down, Martini's Italian Market and the Public Library and Historical Society. And all the other places I now loved and thought of as home.

After a week filled with so much excitement, it was wonderful to sense the deep peacefulness that reigned in Carmine. From now on, my life would be blissfully simple, my biggest challenge learning how to make a killer cannoli.

A police cruiser pulled over to the curb in front of us. The driver's door opened and Anthony stepped out.

Maybe not just cannoli. Maybe also a bit of romance.

"I'll leave you to your date," Roberta said. And she gave me a nod. "Glad we got a happy ending, after all."

"Not an ending, Roberta, but a beginning. A new beginning."

I opened the door and jumped out of the mail truck. I called out Anthony's name. He waved at me, smiling, holding up two cups of takeout coffee.

Our first morning date.

And not, if I had my way, our last.

∼

Thank you so much for visiting Carmine. Join Bernie and her friends for another culinary cozy mystery in book 2:

Sambuca, Secrets, and Murder

Oh, and want a FREE short story? Sign up for my newsletter updates on new books and I'll send the free story to you by email:

https://mpblackbooks.com/newsletter/

Finally, if you enjoyed this book, please take a moment to leave a review online. It makes it easier for other readers to find the book. Thanks so much!

Turn the page to read chapter 1 of *Sambuca, Secrets, and Murder* (Book 2)...

26

SAMBUCA, SECRETS, AND MURDER EXCERPT

My glass of white wine shimmered in the candlelight as I raised it. I wanted this night to be special. Maybe it would even end with more than a kiss, if I could get the nerve to invite Anthony Ferrante back to my place.

Anthony—police officer by day, my date tonight, and 24/7 handsome hunk—raised his glass of red.

"To a perfect date."

"And a perfect restaurant," I said.

On a Friday night, Carlo's Restaurant hit all the right notes: elegant white tablecloth with crystal glasses, soft lighting, and a mellow soundtrack mixing 1950s crooners and cool jazz. Carlo had even given us one of the best seats in the house—right by the window overlooking Garibaldi Avenue, Carmine's main street.

But I hadn't mentioned Carlo's simply to make conversation. I was edging the topic toward my next point. I forked another piece of my chicken cacciatore, chewed and swallowed, then took a fortifying gulp of wine.

"Carlo's is cozy," I said, "though I can think of a place that's even cozier..."

I was about to suggest that my little house on Lampedusa Lane was ideal for a nightcap, when a bright light exploded at the corner of my eye, and I dropped my fork and knife.

My heart squeezed tight. What was that? A silent explosion?

Another flash.

I looked out the window and let out a groan. Of course. I should have known. Outside stood a photographer snapping photos, now with the flash on, now without.

Anthony got halfway out of his seat. "*Maron*, I'm going to—"

"Not tonight." I gestured for him to sit. "I won't let them ruin our date."

Turning to get Carlo's attention, I saw Maria Ferrante, Anthony's sister and waitress at the restaurant, striding across the floor, her menacing glare aimed at the man outside. She stepped past me, grabbed the heavy velvet curtains, and yanked them shut, closing off the view to the outside.

"Those—"

I held up a hand, stopping her before she could impress me with her extensive range of Italian slang.

"It's all right, Maria. Now they won't bother us again."

"You're being very calm," Maria said, and I caught a note of admiration in her voice. "I don't know how you can stomach it. All that public attention would drive me crazy. If I were you, I'd be out there giving that *chooch* a black eye."

"Imagine the headlines if I knocked one of those guys down? They'd love it."

I shrugged, picked up my knife and fork, and casually

speared the last of my chicken, trying hard to keep my hands from shaking. My heart raced. My fingertips tingled, as if thousands of pins were pricking me. It was one thing to say I was calm, quite another to feel it.

"If I keep a cool head," I explained, "eventually they'll lose interest and the whole thing will blow over."

I hoped I was right. Ever since I'd left witness protection, and the media had learned that I was living in Carmine, New Jersey, tabloid journalists had been camped outside my home and outside Moroni's Italian Bakery, where I worked.

Now if you'll only move along, Maria...I need some of that privacy I've been craving, so I can ask your brother back to my place for a nightcap.

"Maybe you're right about staying calm, Bernie. It seems like only a few hardcore paparazzi are still sticking around." Maria put a hand on my arm, giving me a sympathetic look. "Still, a little sambuca will help the nerves. I'll be right back."

A moment later, she'd cleared our plates from the table and returned with a bottle of clear liquor and two shot glasses. Each glass had three coffee beans at the bottom.

"For health, happiness, and prosperity," Maria explained. "Maybe I should add one for love, huh?"

She winked at me.

"That's enough, sis," Anthony said.

She pointed a finger at her brother. "You make sure you treat her good, you hear, Anthony? She's not one of your high-school sweethearts you can fool around with—Bernie's special."

He swiped a hand at her. "Get outta here."

Maria dodged him and blew me a kiss. I watched her saunter away, humming to herself, checking on customers at another table, and my insides warmed at the thought of Maria's compliment.

A few weeks ago, I had thought I would never trust anyone again. I had believed Carmine was a dead end. Now it truly felt like home, with friends all around.

And a bit of romance, too.

Anthony raised his glass of sambuca. "*Salut.*"

I raised mine and drank.

The sweetness of the anise-flavored liquor hit my tongue, and then burned pleasantly as it went down my throat.

"Anthony," I said. "What I wanted to suggest was—"

Anthony's phone pinged in his sport coat, which was slung over the back of his chair. Then pinged again.

"Sorry."

He dug it out and stared at the screen. His lips quirked into a brief smile.

"What is it?" I asked.

"Oh, nothing." He slipped the phone back into his jacket pocket. "Just work."

Anthony and I spent much of our time together talking about work, and when we'd started going on coffee dates, I'd worried he was attracted to me because of our shared interest. Between his day job as a cop and my past career playing a detective on TV—not to mention my incurable curiosity for crime—we never ran out of topics related to law and order.

"You working on a special case?"

He shrugged. "The usual stuff..."

Before I could ask more, Carlo himself came to our table with two dessert plates.

"Dessert is on the house," he said.

Carlo Moroni was a stocky guy with a black goatee.

Tonight he wore a black, tight-fitting turtleneck that accentuated his pot belly.

He set down the plates, and I recognized the pastry.

"That's right—*bomboloni*," he said, smiling at me. "Courtesy of Moroni's Italian Bakery."

Angelica Moroni, my boss and friend, was Carlo's sister, and they often collaborated, with the bakery providing a daily supply of cannolis to the restaurant. I knew Angelica had been making a batch of bomboloni, but I had yet to try them. I was sure I would love them. They were Italian doughnuts filled with cream or jam.

The ones Carlo served, rolled in granulated sugar, contained a chocolate cream. He'd added a dollop of vanilla gelato on the side. Carlo's philosophy of food seemed to be "more is better."

I bit into my bomboloni. The soft dough, the crunch of sugar, the rich chocolate—I closed my eyes and let out a long, drawn-out "Yum..."

Anthony's eyes shone with pleasure as he chewed. He smiled. I smiled. Now was a good time.

"After dessert," I said, "how about we—"

"Bernie Smyth—or should I say, 'Eve Silver'?"

Mamma mia, how many interruptions could I suffer?

Two ladies in their seventies—Sofia Ruggiero and Rose Calabrese—crowded around me. I knew Sofia from Martini's Italian Market, and I'd heard Rose was her best friend, and that both of them were enthusiastic poker players.

"I loved you as Eve Silver on *Silver & Gold*," Sofia said. "My favorite show."

"And I loved you in the Jay Casanova trial," Rose said, her croaky voice suggesting decades of breathing through a cigarette. "I saw you on Court TV with Jay Casanova. I tell you that boy, that *disgraziad*, he sure got what he deserved." She tsk-tsked. "Drugs and guns—who would've thought…"

Everyone had been surprised. I'd caught Jay Casanova, my co-star on *Silver & Gold*, and America's top showbiz heartthrob, smuggling drugs and guns. My cooperation with the DEA and testimony in court had sent him to prison—and because of the threat of revenge, forced me into witness protection. But Jay and his brother, Harry, had failed to get back at me. So I could stop worrying and begin living my new, normal life.

Rose leaned closer. "By the way, I read in *The Hollywood Buzz* that now you're out of witness protection, you could change back to your old name. So, what'll it be—you going back to being Bernadette Kovac again?"

I shook my head. "I like Bernie Smyth. It's an ordinary name for an ordinary life."

Rose gave her friend a raised eyebrow. "See?"

"Fine, you win," Sofia grumbled, and handed over a five-dollar bill.

They walked toward the exit, and I smiled. It was nice to know the locals supported me.

"So, Anthony, as I was suggesting," I said—and then gasped. A young man barreled through the entrance to Carlo's. He shoved his way past Sofia and Rose. Sofia teetered on her high heels, her arms wheeling. She fell.

This time, I was the one leaping up. In an instant, I was by Sofia's side, helping her to her feet.

"Thanks, angel. No broken bones."

She smoothed out her dress and glared over at the man who'd knocked her down.

"What kind of *mamaluke*—"

Her eyes widened. She put a hand on her friend's arm.

"Rose, isn't that—?"

"It is, Sofia. It is."

The restaurant goers had gone quiet. The soundtrack, a high, twanging jazz guitar backed by the low whomp of a bass, so atmospheric a moment ago, now felt out of place.

Everyone's eyes were on the newcomer. The guy must have been in his late twenties. He had sharp, angular features and black, greasy hair. There was no doubt about his persona. He was a leather-jacket-wearing bad boy, and would easily have fit into the cast of *The Outsiders*.

"So this is where the saints of Carmine come to eat," he said, staring disdainfully at his surroundings. "I see things haven't changed much."

"Johnny Greco."

Maria had come out of the kitchen bearing two plates with dessert—more bomboloni with ice cream. But seeing the guy, Johnny, she'd come to a stop. Her face was twisted in a grimace.

"Johnny Greco," she repeated, as if she couldn't believe it. Then she seemed to steel herself for a confrontation. "Last time I saw you was on the front page of the newspaper after you set fire to your parents' house. What have you come back for? What do you want?"

Johnny swaggered over to an empty table. He plonked down on a seat and thrust his muddy boots up on the chair next to it.

"Lasagna will do." Obviously, that hadn't been what Maria was asking about. Johnny looked around. "What's everyone staring at? Anyone got a problem with me eating dinner at Carlo's oh-so-fancy restaurant?"

Anthony shot to his feet.

"If your parents hadn't dropped those charges…"

"And the old chief of police hadn't been a friend of my

dad's?" Johnny laughed. "Yeah, funny how things work in Carmine. Is the police force still as corrupt as always?"

Anthony took a step forward, his fists clenched. But Maria gave her brother a look of warning, and he must have understood. He stayed where he was.

"You want to eat, Johnny?" Maria said. "Fine. Sit and eat. But we don't want any trouble."

"Who's *we*?"

"Me. Carlo. All of Carmine."

Maria approached him. With a quick movement, she kicked the chair out from under his feet. Johnny's boots hit the floor, and he nearly fell off his seat, grasping the sides of his chair to keep from falling.

"Hey..."

"So," Maria said with a smile as jagged as broken glass. "What can I get you, Mr. Greco?"

"Mr. Greco is my dad," Johnny mumbled, the corners of his mouth turning down. "And I told you, I want lasagna. And gimme a beer, too."

"I'll be back shortly with your beer, little boy. Until then, sit still, and don't disturb anyone. *Capisce*?"

I was impressed by how Maria handled Johnny, whose swagger seemed to cover a childish petulance.

Anthony sat down again. His shoulders were tensed, and he glowered as he poured and downed a shot of sambuca.

Maria arrived with a bottled beer and a glass for Johnny. Without acknowledging Maria, Johnny grabbed the bottle and took a swig.

"Ah," he said. "That's good."

Then he looked at Anthony.

"I drove all the way from California on my bike. Real road trip. You know, like Jack Kerouac. You ever read *On the*

Road, Anthony? I bet you didn't. I heard you became a cop. Do cops even read books?"

This guy was an obnoxious brat, and I couldn't stand it any longer.

"*On the Road*? You mean the Willie Nelson song?" I winked at Anthony. "Or maybe you were inspired by Jon Bon Jovi's cross-country trip and the song that came out of it, *Dry County*. A Jersey classic."

Johnny frowned. "Who's this comedian?"

Then his eyebrows lifted. Great. Of course he'd recognize me.

"Well, well, well. If it isn't Bernadette Kovac, the famous missing actress, who isn't missing anymore. I should've guessed you were here. I saw the paparazzi outside."

"Never mind me," I said. "Why don't you tell us why you've come back to Carmine? Judging by the big performance you're putting on, I'm guessing you're dying to tell everyone. Isn't that why you came to Carlo's? For an audience?"

This got me a glare.

"It's none of your business."

"Then you won't mind if we all eat our dinners and don't talk to you."

Johnny seethed for a moment, and I thought he was going to let us get back to our dessert. Then he said, "Fine. You want to know so badly? I'll tell you. I came back because there are truths that need to be told. Secrets that have been buried too long. It's those secrets that fester and make people sick with hypocrisy." He drained his beer. I thought I heard him mumble, "Including myself."

He snapped his fingers at Maria. "Another."

Maria brought him another beer and then left for the kitchen. The rest of the restaurant still seemed to hold its breath. Frankly, I was amazed this twerp commanded such awe or fear—was he such a bad seed?

Johnny took a swig of his beer. He wiped his mouth with the back of his hand.

"I came back to get clean. To scrub off the dirt." Johnny smiled at Maria as she returned with a plate of steaming lasagna. "Speaking of dirt, Maria. The secrets I could tell about you..."

Maria glared down at him.

"You know nothing about me, Johnny Greco, nothing these people want to hear."

"Oh, I know..."

"Like how when we were teenagers, we kissed behind the high school gym? Like how we smoked cigarettes in recess? I'm sure everyone's got more important things to talk about."

"But it's exactly who you kissed in high school that I'm talking about. Except it wasn't a student you were kissing."

Maria visibly tensed. Her eyes widened and her mouth worked, as if she wanted to fire back and answer, but the words wouldn't come.

Johnny saw her surprise, too, because his smile broadened. He leaned back in his chair, obviously enjoying the moment.

"You didn't think I knew that. But I kept a record of everything—all the gossip and rumors and discoveries I made—everything written down. Your little romance is one of the many shocking secrets that Carmine has kept under wraps. I can't wait to see what people say when they hear about the affair you had in high school...with a teacher." He turned to the other patrons in the restaurant, making sure his audience was listening. It was. "Maria dumped me, because she got the hots for a teacher. And that teacher's name was—"

He let out a yelp. Maria had dumped the plate with hot lasagna onto his lap. He scrambled to his feet and batted at his crotch with his hands, trying to get the scalding food off. The result was that he did a little dance, and a few of the patrons laughed.

He stared at Maria, bug-eyed with surprise and anger.

"That burned me," he complained.

Maria stepped up to him and stuck a finger in his face.

"Listen to me, and listen to me good, little Johnny. You're a good for nothin' *stunad*. If you so much as peep about my past—or anyone else's—I will wring your neck and bash in your head. You hear?"

Johnny stared at her.

Then, calmly, Maria turned to Anthony. "Officer Ferrante, I believe this customer has caused a public disturbance. Would you mind escorting him outside?"

"With pleasure," Anthony said and shot to his feet, a grim smile on his face as he rolled up his sleeves.

He grabbed Johnny's arm.

But Johnny tore himself free.

"Don't touch me."

He pushed past Anthony, then paused by our table, right next to me. He didn't look at me. Instead, he eyed the bottle of sambuca. In a flash, he'd grabbed it off the table, and then stomped out of the restaurant.

He left a heavy silence in his wake.

Anthony dropped back into the seat across from me. He sighed and ran a hand through his hair. Then his phone pinged again. He dug it out, read something on the screen, and then tapped away, as if writing a text message.

"Good riddance," Maria said.

She made the gesture of brushing her hands free of dirt, and then strode to the bar, where she changed the music from calm jazz to upbeat Louis Prima and yanked up the volume.

Suddenly, the restaurant felt lively.

Carlo, apparently approving of the solution, stepped into the middle of the room and spread out his arms.

"Sambuca for everyone—it's on the house!"

People clapped, though the applause was probably as much for Maria's benefit as for Carlo's generosity. As the atmosphere grew more festive, I took a deep breath.

No more interruptions. I had a dozen questions about this Johnny Greco guy, but they could wait. Anthony and I could talk later—on my couch.

Over the din of music and talking, I said, "Anthony, how about coming back to my place for a nightcap?"

He put away his phone and leaned forward. He put a hand over mine, and my heart leaped into my throat.

Yes, I thought. *Yes.*

"Sorry, Bernie, no," he said, shaking his head. "It's been a crazy night, and I've gotta get up early in the morning."

No?

Want more? Keep reading book 2:
Sambuca, Secrets, and Murder

MORE BY M.P. BLACK

A Wonderland Books Cozy Mystery Series
A Bookshop to Die For
A Theater to Die For
A Halloween to Die For
A Christmas to Die For

An Italian-American Cozy Mystery Series
The Soggy Cannoli Murder
Sambuca, Secrets, and Murder
Tastes Like Murder
Meatballs, Mafia, and Murder

Short stories
The Italian Cream Cake Murder

ABOUT THE AUTHOR

M.P. Black writes fun cozies with an emphasis on food, books, and travel—and, of course, a good old murder mystery.

In addition to writing and publishing his own books, he helps others fulfill their author dreams too.

M.P. Black has lived in many places, including Austria, Costa Rica, and the United Kingdom. Today, he lives in Copenhagen, Denmark, with his family.

Join M.P. Black's free newsletter for updates on books and special deals:

https://mpblackbooks.com/newsletter/

Made in the USA
Coppell, TX
13 September 2024